PURRFECTLY ROYAL

THE MYSTERIES OF MAX 13

NIC SAINT

PUSS IN PRINT PUBLICATIONS

PURRFECTLY ROYAL

The Mysteries of Max 13

Copyright © 2019 by Nic Saint

Edited by Chereese Graves

www.nicsaint.com

Give feedback on the book at: info@nicsaint.com

facebook.com/nicsaintauthor
@nicsaintauthor

First Edition

Printed in the U.S.A

CHAPTER 1

It had been a rough night so far, cat choir a disastrous experience. Shanille, our conductor, had the gall to tell me, and in front of the whole group, too, if you please, that I sang so much out of tune that either I took private lessons to improve my singing, or she was going to kick me out of cat choir altogether.

Apparently—and this is only hearsay so take it with a grain of kibble—two members had complained. They were cats standing in my immediate vicinity, claiming that I sang so loud and so pitchy they had trouble singing in tune themselves, and as a consequence the performance of all the tenors suffered.

Harriet, of course, thought the whole thing hilarious, and had laughed heartily. She, a prominent member of the sopranos, didn't have to worry about her position and standing, and obviously didn't care a hoot that I did.

"But I don't sing out of tune!" I cried in feeble protest, knowing full well that the damage was done and the minds of fellow choir members made up.

Shanille looked hesitant. She doesn't like disciplining people, but she has a choir to run, and choirs are like leashes: they're only as strong as their weakest link—or is that chains? At any rate, evidently that weakest link was me.

"Okay," she finally said, relenting. Possibly for the dear old friendship we shared. "Sing after me." And she proceeded to intone one of the harder songs on our repertoire, a vocal run I'd never particularly liked or enjoyed singing.

"Ooh-aah-eeh-aah-ooh-aah-aah," she sang. Beautifully, I might add.

So I repeated the exact same run, only in a lower register. I also closed my eyes, as I'd seen Mariah Carey do, and I adopted the way she likes to touch her ear when she sings. I like to think it makes me look like a professional. But when I opened my eyes, the first thing I saw was Shanille's frown.

I gave her my best smile. "How did I do? Blew you away, right?"

"With a wrecking ball," commented Milo, one of my least favorite choir members.

Shanille swallowed nervously. "Maybe give it another shot, Max," she said encouragingly. "And this time keep your eyes open and focus on me."

I could see where she was coming from. After all, what good is a choir conductor if the choir members won't even bother keeping her in their sights? Only problem is, I feel more in control and able to focus better on my singing when I'm not distracted by the others. But seeing as this was one of those do-or-die moments, I decided not to play hardball but acquiesce instead.

"Ooh-aah-eeh-aah-ooh-aah-aah," I sang with feeling.

Judging from the way Shanille winced, it was not my best work.

And when the final note had died away, she spoke those

fateful words: "Max, I think you should find a private tutor, and only come back when you've improved to a spectacular degree."

"But, Shanille!"

To no avail. I could tell from the way she curled her upper lip she wasn't budging.

"I'm sorry, Max. I have the other members to think about."

I let my gaze glide pleadingly over the faces of these other members, most of whom I'd known for years, many who were my bestest, closest friends. Like Dooley, and Brutus, and Harriet. But all I got in return were blank looks. And then Dooley said, "I can tutor you, Max."

"I don't think so, Dooley," said Shanille before I had a chance to respond. "But thanks for the offer."

"I could tutor him," said Brutus, a little gruffly.

"You're a bass, Brutus," Shanille pointed out. "You can't tutor a tenor."

"Why don't I tutor him?" Harriet suggested. But then the meaning of Shanille's words got through to her, and she added, "Oh, but I'm a soprano, so that's probably a no-no, right?"

"I'm a tenor," said Milo. "Though I doubt whether a private tutor will do him any good. Singing is one of those talents you either possess or don't possess, and clearly Max doesn't have what it takes to be a singer."

"Milo," said Brutus warningly, taking my side. It warmed my heart.

"I'm only saying this to help you, Max," Milo said. "No offense, buddy, but you're probably better off finding yourself a different hobby. Whittling, for instance. You could bring a lot of beauty into this world by whittling, Max."

"I don't whittle," I said, trying to put a growl into my

voice and failing miserably. I'm not a natural growler. And apparently not a singer either.

"Max," said Shanille. "I'd teach you myself, but since I'm busy, busy, busy…"

I nodded morosely. I could see which way the wind was blowing, and it definitely wasn't blowing in my direction.

"It's fine," I said. "I'll just… go, I guess."

And so I started moving away. I sorta, kinda hoped multiple voices would ring out clamoring, "No, Max, don't go! Cat choir just isn't the same without you!"

But no voices rang out in the night at all. None whatsoever. Instead, the moment my back was turned, choir practice recommenced as if nothing had happened. Then, suddenly, as I walked off, head low and my spirits even lower, I became aware of a presence next to me. When I looked up, I saw that it was Dooley.

"I'd still like to be your tutor, Max," he said. "I think I could help you."

"Thanks, Dooley," I said. "But you don't have to do this."

"It's fine," he said. "Cat choir isn't much fun without you there."

It touched my heart to such an extent I actually teared up. "Thanks, Dooley," I said brokenly. "That means a lot to me, buddy."

"I'll help you, too," said a second voice. It was Brutus. "I know I'm a bass and you're a tenor, but I'll do what I can to make you rise to my level. It won't be easy, of course, as I'm such an excellent singer, but I'll give it my best shot."

"Gee, thanks, Brutus," I said, strangely touched by his words.

"And my offer still stands," a third voice spoke. Harriet gave me a meaningful smile. "I'm sure together we'll make you a singer yet, Max."

We walked on in silence for a few beats, then I said, "Am I really as bad as all that?"

When they didn't reply, but instead exchanged knowing glances, I had my answer. Yup. That was the night I learned what a terrible singer I really am!

Hopefully, though, with a little help from my friends, I'd overcome this affliction.

CHAPTER 2

*C*hase woke up and blinked. He lay there, eyes wide open, wondering if it was time to get up. Judging from the fact that it was still dark out, it wasn't. And a glance at his bedside clock told him it was two o'clock. At night.

And then he heard it. Cats mewling and yowling and producing the kinds of sounds only cats can make.

His lips twitched in amusement.

He'd recently learned that his girlfriend, Odelia Poole, possessed the rare and wonderful ability of being able to talk to cats. And those same cats could actually hear her and understand what she was saying!

It all seemed fantastical to him, and he'd never have believed it if he hadn't seen it with his own two eyes and heard it with his own two ears.

The only unfortunate aspect of the whole thing was that he wasn't able to learn how to do it himself. He'd asked Odelia to teach him the language but she'd told him it wasn't really a language but more of a mystical connection she and her mother and grandmother seemed to have with the feline species.

Fair enough, but he still wished he possessed the same mystical connection, only maybe with dogs not cats. He loved dogs. Had always loved dogs. And just the idea that he would be a proud dog owner—or the dog the proud owner of him!—and that he could talk to the adorable mutt would be so great.

He rubbed his face as he listened to the protracted wails and screeches.

Odelia, of course, would know exactly what they were talking about, but one look at her tousled blond head told him she was still sound asleep.

His curiosity getting the better of him, he padded over to the window and looked out into the night. A full moon lit up the backyard of the house he now shared with Odelia, and sure enough, four cats sat gathered in the postage stamp of a lawn, screeching and screaming their hearts out. As far as he could tell they were just making noise, but who was he kidding? For all he knew they were discussing quantum mechanics or the latest social media scandal.

"They're singing," suddenly a voice sounded from the bed.

He turned around with an amused expression on his face.

Odelia's tousled head had lifted and she was staring at him sleepily, her eyes half-lidded. "*Somewhere over the rainbow, way up high...* Or at least that's what they're trying to sing. They're not great singers, those cats of mine."

He laughed. "Are you seriously telling me they're singing a song?"

"Yup. They go to cat choir every night, which is more of an excuse to get together and socialize than to perform in Madison Square Garden one day."

"Hey, I like to sing," he said. "Maybe I can join them?"

"Be my guest," she said, and lay back down. "But leave me out of it, will you? I have to work tomorrow and I need my eight hours."

He needed his eight hours, too, but one night of reduced slumber wouldn't hurt, so he slipped his feet into his slippers and went downstairs to join the fearsome foursome as they traded notes and massacred *Over The Rainbow.*

"Hey, guys," he said as he walked out into the night, and cinched the sash of his bathrobe around his muscular form. "Would you mind if I joined you?"

The cats meowed something he didn't understand, but it didn't sound hostile, so he dragged out a lawn chair and sat down. Then Max seemed to hold up a paw as if to count to three, and he bobbed his head in sync with his motions, then the cop and the four cats all broke into song.

"Somewhere over the rainbow, way up high..."

Suddenly a window was thrown open from the next house and a head poked out.

"Will you cut it out with all the noise!"

It was Odelia's grandmother, and she did not look pleased.

"It's not noise!" he shouted back. "The cats and I are singing!"

"Go 'sing' someplace else," she said. "You're waking up the whole neighborhood with your horrible caterwauling."

He shook his head, and saw that Max was shaking his head, too.

"True talent is never appreciated, is it?" he said.

And he could have sworn that Max answered in the affirmative.

In defiance of his future grandmother-in-law, he opened his mouth to belt out a few more bars, and this time a window opened on the other side of the house, and a boot swished through the air and hit him on the back of the head.

"Hey!" he said.

"Oh, be quiet!" a voice yelled. He couldn't see who it was, but assumed it was Odelia's next-door neighbor Kurt

Mayfield. A retired music teacher, apparently the singing didn't appeal to his finely honed musical sensibilities.

It wasn't the first time Chase had been chastened by critical responses to his singing. He directed a quizzical look at Max and the others. "How do you guys deal with this boot-throwing business? Does this happen a lot?"

The four cats lifted their shoulders as if to say: 'Welcome to our world, buddy.'

A window now opened above him and Odelia's sleepy head poked out. "When I said it's fine for you to join them I didn't think you'd actually go through with it. Do you know what time it is?" She yawned for emphasis.

"I just figured I'd spend some bonding time with your cats," he said.

"Yeah, well, I hate to break it to you, Chase, but you can't sing—and you guys can't sing either," she added when a questioning meow came from Dooley. "Better get back inside before the neighbors call the cops on you."

"Hey, wouldn't that be something? I'd have to arrest myself for disturbing the peace."

"Go back to bed, Chase."

"Yeah, go back to bed, Chase!" a voice sounded from next door. It was the same tetchy neighbor.

Then Gran chimed in, "Do what your girlfriend tells you to, Chase!"

"Okay, fine," he said. He eyed the four cats keenly, and thought they were smiling at him. "So it was great spending time with you guys," he said, and held up his hand. They actually high-fived him!

"Hey, did you see that?" he asked, but Odelia had already returned to bed.

"Let's go inside, buddies," he said. "And do some more singing tomorrow."

They moved into the house, single file, and the night was still once more.

CHAPTER 3

I woke up the next morning in an unfamiliar but pleasant position: face to face with Chase, of all people. Usually I wake up having cuddled my way up to Odelia, but apparently Chase has grown on me for me to favor him. My friends were all in various positions on the bed: Dooley was butt to butt with Odelia, while Harriet and Brutus were entangled at the foot of the bed.

Odelia has joked in the past that she would probably have to buy a bigger bed at some point to accommodate her expanding household, and I guess that wouldn't be such a bad idea. For one thing, my paw was dangling over the precipice, one bump from Chase enough to send me over the edge myself.

He woke up with a loud snore and stared at me. I stared right back and smiled. "Hey, there, sleepyhead," I said by way of greeting.

He blinked a few times, then said, "Odelia? Your cat is staring at me!"

"He's showing you how much he cares," she muttered.

"I do care about you, Chase," I said earnestly. I happen to

think Chase is the bee's knees—he and Odelia a match made in heaven.

Chase looked a little ill at ease. He's not used to waking up being stared at by a cat. It's a sign of affection, as Odelia had correctly surmised, and to show him I really liked him, I put my paw on his face and gently dabbed his nose.

He swallowed, as he lay there, frozen like a popsicle. Weird.

"Relax, Chase," she said. "He's not going to eat you."

"Yeah, but he might scratch me in the face."

"He won't. Max is very careful not to use his claws."

I am. I don't like to scratch my humans. They tend to bleed. Such sensitive creatures. Sometimes, of course, I can't help it, like when I'm excited about a rare treat. I wasn't now —just feeling happy.

"Max," said Chase. "Please don't scratch me. I like my face the way it is."

"I like your face, too," I said. "It's a nice face, as faces go."

Dooley, who'd woken up, said, "Oh, are you having a tête-à-tête with Chase? I'll join you." He crawled over Odelia and got right on top of Chase, then started purring up a storm and kneading the man's stomach.

"Ouch!" said Chase.

"No claws, Dooley," said Odelia.

"Let me get in there, you guys," said Harriet, and plunked herself gracefully down on Chase's chest, making herself comfortable.

"I feel left out," said Brutus.

"There's still a spot near his head," I pointed out.

"Great," muttered Brutus, and draped himself across Chase's head.

Now four cats were purring up a storm, and kneading our new favorite human. Chase has saved my life numerous times, and Dooley even thinks he might be Jesus. I wouldn't go as far as that, but he is a pretty solid dude, in my humble opinion, and cats, even though they're rumored to stint on the emotion, are actually very emotional creatures, and like to show their affection rather than jabber on and on about it like some other species.

Plus, Chase had sung with us last night, and even taken a boot to the head for his trouble. How cool was that?

Odelia finally managed to drag her eyelids high enough to warrant eyesight, and laughed when she saw the predicament her boyfriend was in.

"You're now officially owned by four cats," she said, shaking with laughter.

"I feel pretty... funny," he said.

"Ooh, I know that song!" said Harriet. "*I feel pretty. Oh so pretty.*"

And soon we were all singing at the top of our lungs, Odelia was laughing, and even Chase had to chuckle—very carefully, though. Hard to chuckle with four cats hampering your chuckling movements.

Just then, a voice rang out from downstairs.

"Are you two lovebirds up yet?"

Chase and Odelia exchanged a glance. "Gran," they said in unison.

"Come on up, Gran!" Odelia yelled.

"Wait, no," said Chase, but too late.

Already feet could be heard pounding up the stairs, and moments later a little old white-haired lady burst through the door. When she saw Chase loaded with cats, she laughed. "Well, now ain't that a sight for sore eyes!"

"Ha ha ha," said Chase, but I could tell his heart wasn't in it. His next words proved this. "What do you want, Vesta?"

Her smile vanished. "Be nice to your granny-in-law, mister," she growled.

"You insulted my singing last night! Called it cater-wauling!"

"I was only trying to offer you a learning opportunity. How do you two feel about a trip to England?"

"England?" said Odelia, staring at her grandmother.

"It's a country. In Europe."

"I know what England is. Why would we go on a trip there?"

"Why not? You remember Angela? Angela Torrance?" When Odelia shook her head, she added, "When I tell you she's the mother of Tessa Torrance?"

"Oh, that Angela," said Odelia, nodding.

"Who's Angela Torrance?" I asked.

"She lived around the corner for a while and was great friends with Mom," said Odelia. "Gran used to babysit her daughter Tessa—we're the same age."

"Tessa Torrance as in *the* Tessa Torrance?" asked Chase. "The princess?"

"Technically she's not a princess, even though she married a prince," said Gran. "The English are weird like that. Anyway, I got a call from Angela just now. There was an incident with her daughter and she wants us to go over there and find out what's going on."

"Incident?" asked Odelia. "What kind of incident?"

"A big stone almost crushed her. She's lucky to be alive."

"But... don't they have cops in England?"

"They do. But Tessa wants to keep the whole thing quiet. She told her husband Prince Dante it was an accident but she's not too sure herself. And now she wants us to investigate. Isn't that great?!"

"But..."

"What's with all the buts? Don't you want a free European vacation?"

"Of course I do, but I don't see—"

"Look, Angela has read all about your sleuthing adventures, and she's told Tessa about it, and now they want you to go over there to keep an eye on things. Is that so hard to understand?"

"But…" She ignored Gran's expressive groans of frustration. "I can't just waltz in there and start snooping around. Doesn't she have protection officers and royal guards and Scotland Yard or whatever?"

"I told you. She doesn't trust anyone."

"You didn't tell me that."

"Well, I'm telling you now. Angela will arrange everything. You will pretend to be Tessa's cousin, and I'm her grandmother."

"Her grandmother!"

"What? You don't think I can pull it off?"

"Oh, Gran. This sounds like a really bad idea."

"No, it doesn't. It sounds like a great idea. Now get up and get ready. No time to waste."

"Does Prince Dante know?" asked Chase.

"No, he doesn't. Like I said, Tessa doesn't trust anyone."

"Not even her own husband?"

"Hey, I'm just the messenger here, singer boy."

"What about us?" I asked.

Gran grinned widely. "Surprise! You're all invited, too!"

"We are?!"

"I told Angela that you're Odelia's secret power. That she feels she can't do a proper job without her cats by her side."

"Like her talisman?" said Dooley.

"Exactly!" Gran cried. "You're Odelia's talisman, so Angela is going to arrange for all of you to be flown out there, too. On a private jet, no less."

"Do you know what this means?" said Harriet excitedly. "We're going to see the Queen!"

"And her corgis!" said Brutus.

"Who wants to see a corgi?" I said.

"What's a corgi, Max?" asked Dooley.

"A dog. The Queen is crazy about them."

"What are they talking about?" asked Chase.

"They're talking about the corgis," said Odelia. "They're not sure if they're going to like them."

"Of course you're going to like the Queen's corgis," said Chase, patting me in an exaggerated fashion. I can always tell a dog person from a cat person. A dog person pats you as if they're trying to stomp you into the ground. A cat person is gentle and strokes you with delicate movements. I wasn't going to hold it against him, though. The man was obviously on a learning curve.

Odelia quirked an eyebrow. "Well, then. Looks like we're going to England."

We all yipped. Oh, if only I'd known then what I know now!

CHAPTER 4

Suddenly everything had to move fast. Angela Torrance had insisted there wasn't a moment to lose, as her daughter was apparently in grave danger, and she needed Odelia and her sleuthing skills in England now, right speedily!

Odelia had already packed her bag, and so had Chase, and she was now thinking about what to bring along for her cats.

"No worries," said Gran, waving an impatient hand. "Angela said she'd take care of everything."

"That's very generous of her," said Odelia's mother Marge, who was overseeing proceedings.

"But they need their litter boxes and their favorite food and—"

"What they need is their humans," said Gran. "The rest will be provided by Tessa. The best of the best of the best. Angela's words, not mine."

Chase, who sat following the back-and-forth with an indulgent smile, said, "I like the best of the best of the best."

"Yeah, the best of the best of the best is good enough for me," Max agreed.

The doorbell sang out a cheerful tune and Gran got up from the bed on which she'd been lounging. Odelia's bags were on the floor near the door, and as Gran stomped down the stairs, she announced loudly, "That'll be Angela!"

"Oh, dear," said Marge, bringing a worried hand to her face. "Are you sure you want to go through with this, honey?"

"I guess so," said Odelia, though she had her reservations. Especially about the fact that her grandmother was in charge, which usually spelled disaster.

"This Angela seems like a reasonable enough person," said Max as he placed his head on his paws.

"She does," said Odelia. "But we have no idea where we're going to end up over there."

"I don't like the fact that this is all so very secretive," said Marge.

"Me neither. But Angela says it's the only way to proceed. She says we can't trust anyone over there."

"Not even Prince Dante?" asked Marge.

"Not even Prince Dante."

"Poor Tessa. I can't imagine how she must be feeling. You remember Tessa, don't you, honey? You two used to play so well together."

"Mom. I was two."

"Of course you were," said Marge distractedly. "Everything was different back then, of course. Angela and Jack were still very much in love. This was before he ran off with that waitress. I remember Angela being very upset about the whole thing. And then she found this great job in Vegas and that's the last I ever heard of her. Well, until the engagement, of course."

They'd all followed the story of Tessa's engagement to Prince Dante with interest. An American girl falling in love with an English prince was a story that sparked the imagination of the nation, and the fact that Tessa and her mom had once been neighbors added to the excitement. So Odelia, Marge and Gran had watched the royal wedding live, fighting sleep not to miss a thing.

There was movement on the stairs, and moments later Gran reappeared, followed by Angela Torrance. She was a dark-haired, petite woman with a kind face. She smiled when she saw Marge, opening her arms in greeting.

"Angela!" said Marge warmly. "I'm so glad to see you! How have you been?"

"Well, other than the fact that my daughter is being targeted by some crazy killer I can't complain," said Angela with a wry little chuckle.

"I'm so sorry," said Marge as the two women hugged.

"So how come the story hasn't been in all the papers?" asked Odelia.

"Tessa deliberately kept it out," said Angela. "She was fortunate none of the tabloids picked it up. Otherwise it would be all over the news by now."

"But wouldn't that be a good thing?" asked Marge. "That way the killer will think twice before he tries again."

"I'm not so sure about that," said Angela. "The English tabloids have all turned on her, the poor girl, and they'd probably applaud the killer. In fact they just might offer a reward for him to try again and this time do it right."

"Oh, my God," said Marge, shocked by these words.

"Lucky for Tessa she and Dante were the only ones who saw what happened. And one little girl, but she won't talk. Dante went up the roof to check, and he thinks it was an accident: a stone that must have come loose."

"But Tessa doesn't believe that."

"No, she doesn't. And neither do I. Stones don't just drop from the sky. Someone must have used a crowbar to pry it loose and then waited for the right moment to drop it."

Odelia frowned. "But if Dante says—"

"I don't believe him, okay? In fact at this point I don't trust anyone. Not my daughter's husband, not a single person in his family or his entourage. As far as I'm concerned they're all out to get her until proven otherwise."

Odelia was starting to have a bad feeling about this. Angela was more and more coming across as a loose cannon. Surely if Dante said the stone falling was an accident, he was right. Why would he lie about a thing like that?

"Look, the tabloids have created such a frenzied atmosphere..." Angela shook her head. "They've turned Tess's life into a living hell. Everything she does, or says, or even wears—they're ready to crucify her. It's a nightmare."

"But surely Tessa can trust her husband to..." Odelia tried again.

"Don't get me wrong. I like Prince Dante. He's a great guy, and theirs is obviously a match made in heaven. But they've been fighting. Big rows."

"Oh, no," said Marge, who was a romantic soul at heart.

"That doesn't mean he would try to kill her, though," said Odelia.

"I don't know. And that's where you come in. At this point you're the only one I can trust. Vesta told me you have experience solving crime, so..."

"I have experience solving crime in Hampton Cove. I've never even been to England, so I'm not sure what I'll be able to accomplish over there."

"I'm sure you'll handle yourself magnificently," said Angela, and rubbed Odelia's arm encouragingly. She paused. "Look, I can see that you're skeptical about this. So let me show you something." She took out her phone. "I told you the only witnesses were Dante and a little girl, right?"

"Uh-huh."

"The girl just happened to be filming when that stone ball

dropped down." She held up the phone and everyone gathered around to watch. "Look closely."

Odelia looked closely. The shaky footage showed Tessa, standing in front of a gray stone wall. Suddenly, she looked up, then immediately jumped to the left. Moments later, a large solid object dropped down and the camera panned up. On the wall right over Tessa's head, a dark figure could fleetingly be seen. One second he was there, the next he was gone.

"Oh, my God," said Marge.

"Right?" said Angela.

"Did Tessa show this to Dante?"

"She wanted to, but I told her not to. If he's in cahoots with this stone-pusher, he won't be happy that his little scheme was thwarted, not to mention that his associate was caught on film. Better to wait and see what he's up to next. If he's behind this whole thing, we want to catch him red-handed."

"What about the girl?"

"Tessa told her not to mention the incident to anyone."

"Oh, dear," said Marge. "This is terrible, Angela. Tessa must be terrified."

"Honey, why do you think I want to get over there lickety-split? My little girl is all alone, not a single ally in her corner. Well, except for her cousin."

"Her cousin?" asked Odelia.

"Yeah, her real cousin. Nesbit spent his gap year in London, fell in love and married the girl of his dreams a couple of years ago. He's a cop, and Tessa managed to get him assigned to her security detail. We're hoping he'll keep her safe until we arrive."

What a story, Odelia thought. Poor Tessa. And poor Angela. Now she understood why they were so keen for reinforcements to arrive.

Angela glanced over to the bed. "So those are your famous cats, huh?"

"I wouldn't exactly call us famous," said Max, though he was already swelling with pride.

"You write about them all the time," Angela explained, "so I almost feel like I know them."

"They're quite the sleuthhounds," said Gran. "Or should I say sleuthcats?"

Angela didn't laugh. Instead, she gave them all a grave look.

"My daughter is in mortal danger," she said. "Please promise me you'll do whatever you can to catch this maniac."

Odelia placed her hand on the woman's arm and noticed a distinct tremor. She felt for Angela. As a mother it was terrible to have to watch from thousands of miles away what happened to your daughter in a different land—a different world. "I promise I'll do my absolute level best," she said.

"Thank you," said Angela with a grateful smile. "Now let's go. The jet is fueled and ready to whisk us away to the land of fish and chips."

Max pricked up his ears. "Fish?"

Odelia smiled. She'd been worried about her cats going on such a long trip, but somehow she had a feeling everything was going to be just fine.

CHAPTER 5

I hadn't known what to expect when Odelia told us we were flying to a different continent by airplane. I mean, I've seen plenty of planes on TV, and they always seem very enjoyable. You sit together in a cozy space with a slew of pleasant fellow travelers, are served delicious food by smiling flight attendants, and if you're lucky you get to fall in love with Meg Ryan. If you're unlucky you end up sitting next to a psychopath who threatens to kill your dad if you don't do exactly what he says, but Gran had assured us this was rare, and only happens in Hollywood movies featuring Rachel McAdams.

I, for one, had always been curious about flying, even if the prospect of spending long hours in what basically amounts to a steel tube gave me pause. Then again, I'd always known that day would never come, as Odelia is basically a homebody, and so are Gran, Marge and the rest of the fam.

They like Hampton Cove, where they're born and raised, and don't venture too far from the homestead and definitely not to other continents. So now that the day had actually come, I greeted it with a mixture of anticipation and trepidation. Anticipation at the chance of being seated next to Meg Ryan's cat, trepidation at the prospect of spending the flight in the company of Passenger 57 with Wesley Snipes nowhere in sight, if you catch my drift.

As we were driven to the airport by a very kind and buff individual in a Range Rover, Odelia and Chase and Gran made pleasant conversation throughout. They peppered Angela with questions, ranging from her daughter's diet and workout plan to the place where Tessa and Dante had settled down. Apparently this was some sort of cottage on the outskirts of London, close to a castle. Newtmore Cottage, if I understood correctly.

It struck me as odd. I mean to say, who in their right mind, when in the possession of unlimited funds and a vast real estate portfolio, would want to spend the best years of his or her married life in a dank cottage overrun with newts? I guess that's the English for you. They are different from the rest of us.

Too bad Angela was there, or I would have bombarded Odelia with questions myself. As it was, we had a strict rule that when in the company of strangers, Odelia didn't talk to us, and neither did Gran or Marge. You can probably see why. Most people think it strange when other humans start meowing. It often ends in tears and a one-way trip to the looney bin, strapped in a straitjacket. For those of you not in the know, a straitjacket is a special garment worn by those who've lost their marbles. Meaning they're nuts.

The trip to the airport was uneventful, and when we arrived the car was directed to a parking space reserved only for those deserving special treatment. And so, all of a sudden, we'd been transformed into VIPs!

"I think I'm going to like this," said Dooley.

"I think so, too," I said as a muscular man in a snazzy suit and sunglasses gestured to a plane that stood waiting on the tarmac. It was small, it was sleek, and it looked absolutely fabulous.

Odelia and the others were chatting with some sort of official-looking individual, handing him their passports and documents. He cast a quick glance over to us, as we sat on the tarmac in our respective pet carriers, and I hoped he wouldn't tell Odelia we couldn't come along. Gran had been surfing the internet and had discovered England, on account of the fact that it is an island, has some pretty strict rules about pets being brought into the country, and that we needed to have all of our shots and stuff. The mere mention of the word shots was enough to scare the living daylights out of me, but as it turned out we did have the shots we needed to have, and anyway, Angela had made 'arrangements' to make sure we would be allowed into the country.

"Remember that episode with Johnny Depp and his dogs?" asked Harriet now as we sat waiting patiently.

"What episode?" I asked, keeping a keen eye on the person who seemed to have the power to decide our fate.

"Johnny Depp tried to bring his dogs into Australia and when they found out, the politician in charge said he'd murder the dogs if Johnny didn't remove them immediately. They're pretty tough on pets in Australia."

"Oh, my God," said Dooley. "That's terrible!"

"So what did Johnny do?" asked Brutus.

"He filmed a video apologizing to the people of Australia for bringing his dogs into the country and then immediately flew them back to the States."

"I hope the Queen doesn't ask for us to be murdered," said Dooley.

"I don't think so," I said. "Angela said everything has been arranged."

"Angela is not the Queen, Max," said Harriet. "She doesn't get to decide who lives and who dies."

"Must be a tough job," said Brutus. When Harriet shot him a critical look, he added defensively, "Just saying. Deciding who lives or dies? Tough."

"Does she really get to decide if we live or die?" asked Dooley.

"I think so," said Harriet. "England is a monarchy, so the Queen has a lot of pull."

"I'll bet she would never order her corgis to die, though," said Dooley. "She loves those corgis. I saw it on TV."

"I think we need to make friends with the corgis," I said. "That's the only way to make sure we don't get murdered by the Queen. If we make friends with the Queen's favorite pooches, and get them to vouch for us, we're in the clear."

"I'm not going to play nice with a bunch of mutts," said Harriet disdainfully.

"It's either that or death by execution," I said. "Your choice."

"I heard they have peculiar methods of execution," said Brutus. "Like, the gallows? And the ax? Very medieval. And sometimes they lock people up in a place called the Tower of London. Very creepy place. I'll bet it has rats."

I gulped. I did not want to get my head chopped off with an ax. Or get locked up with a bunch of rats for company. "We need to find those corgis and make nice and we need to do it as soon as we arrive," I said.

"I'll bet the Queen's corgis smell of lavender," said Dooley, apropos of nothing.

"What makes you think so?" I asked distractedly, as thoughts of execution by hanging flashed through my mind.

"I don't know. The Queen just looks like a lavender type of person to me, and I'll bet she makes sure her dogs smell nice, like, all the time."

"You're probably right," I agreed. Most mutts smell terrible, but the Queen being a clean and hygienic person would make sure hers smelled wonderful.

"Maybe they smell like roses," said Harriet.

"Or chocolate pudding," said Brutus.

And as we all speculated on what the Queen's corgis smelled like, and thought of ways and means to convince them not to murder us by hanging or removing our heads with an ax, the paperwork seemed to be in order and finally Odelia proceeded in the direction of the airplane, the muscular man stacked our pet carriers onto a trolley and started pushing it in the direction of the plane. It was almost as if we were in bunk beds—a truly novel experience.

"Why do you get to be on top, Max?" lamented Harriet.

"Just happenstance," I said, though I preferred to be on top. I had a nice view, which I didn't think Harriet had from down below on the trolley.

"It's because Max is Odelia's favorite," said Brutus, harking back to a theme he likes to return to from time to time.

"I'm not her favorite," I said. "We're all her favorite."

"She likes you more than the rest of," said Brutus. "Admit it, Max."

"I'm not admitting any such thing. If anything, she likes me less."

"And how do you explain that?"

I didn't. I just wanted to get on top of the argument. "Well..." I began.

"It's because Max is the oldest," said Dooley. "Everybody knows humans prefer the youngest child. They spoil it rotten and the same goes for cats."

"Which would mean that she likes you best," said Harriet.

"Hey, I guess that's true," said Dooley, sounding surprised.

"No, it means she likes me best," said Brutus. "I'm the last one to join the family, so technically that means I'm the youngest child and I'm the favorite."

"I like none of you guys best," Odelia suddenly whispered as she bent down. "I like you all the same. And now will you shut up and enjoy the fun?"

I smiled. "See? She likes us all equally."

"Yeah, yeah," Brutus grumbled. "That's what she wants you to think. She likes me best, and that's a fact."

"I'm the youngest," said Dooley, "so she likes me best."

"But I'm the prettiest," said Harriet, "and it's a proven fact that humans like beautiful babies more than ugly babies. So she likes me best."

"I'm strong," said Brutus. "Humans appreciate strength more than beauty."

And on and on it went. Cats. You can't live with them. You can't kill them.

CHAPTER 6

*L*ike I said, I'd never flown on a plane before, but I'd heard all the horror stories. About cats being locked up in cages in the cargo hold, freezing their tushies off, or being cooked like a lobster. Or even being stowed in the overhead bin only to suffer a claustrophobic episode. So in all honesty I wasn't exactly looking forward to my first experience as a passenger on an airplane.

On the other hand, the alternative was to stay home with Marge and Tex, and go without my favorite human for an unknown length of time, while she whooped it up over in England, solving crime and having a great time with Chase and Grandma and the lavender-smelling corgis.

So... when you're forced to choose between the lesser of two evils, what do you do? Tough one, I know. We'd opted to join the adventure, after a unanimous vote. Harriet was the one most keen to take the plunge, as she'd always wanted to travel to London and see the sights—maybe put in some shopping on Bond Street or Harrods or even spend some time being pampered in some of those fancy pet clinics they have over there, where the rich and famous spoil their pets rotten. Though I pointed out to her that those rich and famous more often than not had dogs, not cats. One of those sad facts of life.

"So we'll be the first," she said stubbornly. "We'll be the avant-garde of a new revolution: out with the pampered dogs and in with the pampered cats!"

"Good luck with that," I said, reminding her she sometimes got seasick riding in the car with Gran.

"That's because Gran is a terrible driver," she snapped. "And I happen to have a very sensitive stomach."

She does have a sensitive stomach. But then she has a sensitive everything.

"I also happen to think I just might have irritable bowel syndrome," she went on.

"More like irritable person syndrome," I said with a light laugh. She would have poked me in the snoot but we were still tucked tightly into our carriers.

The muscular man who'd driven the Range Rover now carried us aboard, along with more muscular men who seemed to be part of a group of muscular men. They all looked similar and I was starting to wonder if they were related.

"Who are all these people?" asked Harriet, as our carriers were deposited on the floor of a spacious cabin that did not look like the interior of all of those airplane movies I'd watched over the years. It looked a lot more luxurious.

"I think they work for Angela's daughter," said Brutus. "Tessa Torrance probably has lots of people working for her now that she's a princess."

"She's not a princess," said Harriet. "She's a duchess. Duchess of Essex."

"What does a duchess of sex do, Max?" asked Dooley.

"Essex," Harriet corrected him. "It's a place in England

where they make reality shows. Or at least that's what Gran told me."

I studied my surroundings. The plane was nicely furnished, with cream-colored ceilings, cream-colored floors, cream-colored leather seats, and cream-colored tables where presumably cream-colored beakers with cream-colored non-alcoholic beverages would be served once we had liftoff. I searched around for a cream-colored bowl and a cream-colored litter box with cream-colored litter but didn't immediately spot one. All in good time, right?

Odelia, Chase and Gran had also come aboard, followed by Angela, who was flying over to England with us.

"Who owns this plane?" asked Odelia as she sat down in one of the snazzy seats and made herself comfortable.

I was frankly dying to take a seat myself, as the leather looked soft as butter and particularly inviting. I would have to refrain from digging my claws in, though. One of those habits that's very hard to kick for a feline.

"It belongs to one of Tessa's friends," said Angela. "A friend whose name may or may not start with a C and end with Looney."

"Mr. Looney?" asked Dooley. "Who's Mr. Looney?"

But we all ignored him, surprise rendering us temporarily mum. Who wasn't mum was Odelia's grandmom. "Oh, my God," she said, taking a seat next to her granddaughter. "Don't tell me we're flying Air Clooney?!"

"Oh, yes, my dear, we are," said Angela.

"Does Mr. C. Looney know why we're flying to England?" asked Odelia.

"Tessa told him she needed to bring her mother and a few of her friends to England as soon as possible, and George immediately offered her his plane."

"Must be nice to have friends like that," said Chase, and he was right.

The door of the plane had finally closed, and Odelia knelt down next to us to check how we were doing.

"I hate these cages, don't you?" I said. "Oh, that's right—presumably you've never been confined to a cage. Well, let me tell you, it's not much fun."

"I'm sorry about this, Max," she said. "But rules are rules."

"Oh, I know all about rules," I assured her. "Like the rule that in order to be a member of cat choir you have to actually be able to sing."

"It's fine," said Harriet. "If that's what it takes to fly to England and join high society, I'll gladly make the sacrifice."

"I'll let you out as soon as the captain gives the sign. You can freely walk the cabin after that—or at least until we land."

"How long until we arrive?" asked Harriet.

"About eight or nine hours," said Odelia. Then she caught Angela's curious glance.

"Don't mind her," said Gran. "She's crazy about those cats."

"Yeah, she pretends to talk to them all the time," said Chase.

"I totally get it," said Angela. "I have a Frenchie back home, and we talk up a storm."

"Why didn't you bring him along?" asked Odelia.

"He's old, and doesn't like to travel as much as he used to. When he was younger I took him everywhere, but now he prefers to stay in his trusted environment." She glanced down at us. "I've never known anyone to travel with cats, though, so that's definitely a first."

"We're all cat ladies," said Gran. "Me, my daughter and granddaughter."

"And I'm an honorary cat lady," Chase quipped.

"That's what happens to the men in our family," said Gran. "It's either join the club or get lost."

Chase laughed. "It's true," he confirmed when Angela quirked a curious eyebrow. "It took some getting used to but now I love them almost as much as Odelia does. They're the cutest little rascals, aren't they?"

And with these words he wiggled his fingers at me.

Odelia placed the carrier next to her and strapped it in, while Gran did the same with Dooley's, and Chase took care of Brutus and Harriet. The pilot announced over the intercom we were cleared by the tower for takeoff, and suddenly my heart started beating so fast I thought it was going to hammer straight through my chest. The engines roared and the plane started moving, then accelerating, with such a mighty roar I suddenly felt awfully faint.

"Max!" Dooley said. "I don't like this!"

"I don't like it either, Dooley!" I cried.

"We're all gonna die!" Brutus said. "This is the end. We're dead!"

"This is what hell looks like," said Harriet. "We've landed in hell!"

The plane hurtled along the runway, at an ever-increasing speed, the noise thundering in my ears, and then, suddenly and without warning, we had liftoff! Without even realizing it, I was screaming at the top of my voice and so were Dooley, Harriet and Brutus.

"Nervous flyer much?" asked Angela with an amused smile.

Odelia had opened the carrier and now hugged me close.

Gran and Chase followed her example, and I could tell Harriet was digging her claws into Chase's thighs for he grimaced and gently removed them.

"It's all right, you guys," said Odelia. "Everything is fine."

"Easy for you to say!" I said. "You're not the one whose guts are being ripped out by Mach speed!"

She laughed. "What do you know about Mach speed?"

"I've seen *Top Gun*! And I don't feel the need for speed!"

The plane was still climbing, but then gradually leveled off.

"The seatbelt sign is switched off and you can now move freely about," a sonorous voice boomed through the intercom.

I glanced around as everyone got up and deposited us to the floor.

"Max?" said Dooley.

"Uh-huh?"

"We're alive!"

I laughed. "Whoo-hoo!"

"You guys!" Harriet cried. "We're on our way to England!"

"Yes, we are!" I said, relieved to have survived the ordeal.

"We're going to meet the Queen!" she yipped.

I didn't know about that, but whoever we were going to meet, it was definitely better than meeting our maker!

CHAPTER 7

*O*delia was checking the shaky footage again of the incident that had led them to board a private jet and fly head over heels to England.

They were well underway, the cats had all settled down on the plush pillows Angela or Mr. C. Looney had been so good to provide, and a flight attendant had brought out snacks for them to nibble on.

Once again she watched as Tessa stood smiling in front of the wall of Newtmore House, as Prince Dante's voice warned her to watch out! Moments later, Tessa jumped clear of the stone ball that would have crushed her.

"Tessa and Dante were in charge of the annual Summer Show," Angela explained. "Some kind of county fair, with a bouncy castle for the kids and a band and lots of great food. Ticket sale proceeds go to charity and Tessa especially had spent a lot of time turning it into a success, which it was."

Odelia replayed the footage. The ball impacted the ground with such force that a dull thud could be heard, followed by Dante rushing in and helping Tessa up.

"If Dante hadn't yelled for her to jump, she would have been crushed," said Angela with a grim twist of the lips.

"And you still think he might be behind this," said Odelia. "That doesn't make sense, Angela."

"It does. The way I see it, they just had this big fight over the kind of people he likes to hang out with. Bunch of losers, if you ask me, but he seems reluctant to remove them from his life. Putting Tessa in harm's way and being the one to save her life would have shifted the balance of power in the relationship to him."

"That seems far-fetched."

Angela threw up her arms. "I don't know what to think here, okay?"

Odelia studied the fleeting image of the figure on the roof. Unfortunately it was impossible to make out features or even size or gender. Just a dark blob, moving away the moment the camera caught him or her.

"Whoever this is, they took an awfully big risk," said Odelia.

"I'm sure they were wearing a disguise—a cloak or something."

"I take it Dante never saw this video?"

"No, he hasn't."

"How determined are you to keep this from getting out?" asked Chase.

"Tessa wants to keep it quiet, and I agree. If word got out there was an attempt on her life, all hell would break loose."

"So maybe that's a good thing? I mean, someone could have seen something."

But Angela shook her head. "We want to keep it under wraps. Tessa is not popular as it is, and this would only incite more hatred and all sorts of nastiness. What she's most afraid of is that a bunch of copycats will pop up and act out other assassination scenarios, this time with fatal consequences."

"I can't believe the English people would tolerate that kind of behavior," said Odelia. "She is married to one of their most popular royals, isn't she?"

"Oh, I guess she's popular enough with the people," Angela agreed. "But she's hated by the tabloids. They'd twist this into something else entirely."

"Like what?"

"Oh, I don't know. They'd probably claim she set this up herself. As a publicity stunt. A way to get attention."

"No way."

"Oh, yes. They're vicious like that."

"That's just terrible," said Odelia.

She couldn't imagine having to live like that—being openly hated and despised with such intensity and relentlessness. "At least the other royals are there to support her," she said. And when Angela gave her a dubious look, she said, "They do support her, don't they?"

"Not really. Her sister-in-law isn't exactly taken with her, and as far as the rest of the family is concerned—they're all a bunch of pretty cold fish, if you ask me. They're not very big on warmth and human affection."

They all stared at Angela, even the cats.

"Like I said," Tess's mother continued with a shrug, "the better policy here is not to trust anyone. Which is exactly what's keeping Tessa safe right now."

"So you think they will try again?" asked Odelia.

Angela's face turned grave. "Oh, they already have."

"Oh, my God," said Odelia, bringing a distraught hand to her face.

"Tessa has a habit of drinking a cup of herbal tea before going to bed, and usually she makes it herself—as she has done all her life. Only lately, what with the baby and her busy life, she's been trusting her staff to handle stuff like that. Last night, when she took a sip from her tea, she noticed a strange taste. Bitter. She immediately thought back to the incident with the stone and my words of caution. So she put down the cup, and poured some tea in a small flask. The rest she dumped down the sink. So when the maid came in later, it looked as if she'd drunk the whole cup. She then asked Nesbit to have it tested. Tessa texted me just before liftoff. The tea was laced with belladonna."

Odelia's jaw dropped. "That's a pretty powerful poison."

"It is. So do you see what I mean about not trusting anyone? Someone made that tea for her—someone close to her—someone on her own staff."

"But if they poisoned her tea, who knows what they'll do next!"

"You have to get her out of there," said Chase. "You have to get her back to the States and make sure she's out of harm's way."

"But that's just it. I can't. She's married to a prominent royal. She can't just skedaddle and disappear for a while. She has to carry on as if nothing happened. And that's where you come in. You're going to have to be there—on the scene—and find out who's doing this to her."

"Are you sure Tessa can trust this Nesbit guy?" asked Odelia.

"He's the only one she can trust. There's absolutely no reason for Nesbit to try and hurt his cousin. And it's good for her to see a friendly face in a sea of hostiles. You have to remember, she's all alone out there—she left behind her family, her friends, her whole life, to go and live with a person she only met months before, and a bunch of strangers, in a high-tension situation, scrutinized by the world and the world's toxic media. She's in a tough spot."

"And? What has Nesbit learned so far?"

"A lot. For one thing, there's plenty of people who want

her dead. He's made a list." She handed a piece of paper to Odelia. "I thought it might help you get started."

Odelia glanced down at the list. She was surprised to find half a dozen people there. "All of these people want Tessa dead?" she asked.

"Oh, I'm sure there are plenty more, but you have to start somewhere."

CHAPTER 8

To our not inconsiderable surprise we weren't staying in a hotel, or even some faraway cottage located down the road from the royal dwelling, but in the actual royal dwelling itself. Odelia was as surprised as we were when we finally arrived at destination's end and it turned out to be Newtmore Cottage.

"We're staying here?" asked Odelia when the car pulled to a stop in front of a slightly weird-looking cottage with a very huge chimney stack on top.

"Yup," Angela confirmed. "I've arranged for you to stay here, so you can keep a close eye on my daughter."

The car doors opened and the humans all got out. We were still in our pet carriers, which apparently was a precaution our driver had insisted upon. The carriers were taken out of the car and placed on the porch.

The front door opened and a red-bearded young man came out whom I immediately recognized as Prince Dante. He looked extremely pleased to see us. "Angela!" he cried, then threw his arms wide and greeted her with such affection I found it very hard to believe he was the one we were here to nab.

Behind him, a young woman appeared. She was smartly dressed in a white cable-knit sweater and black pants and looked absolutely radiant. She was carrying a baby in her arms, and greeted her mother with genuine warmth. When it came time to greet the rest of us, she didn't stint either. "Cousin Odelia!" she said and gave Odelia three kisses. "It's been too long!"

"Yeah, far too long," Odelia agreed.

"And this must be Chase," said Tessa, greeting Chase. "I've never actually met Odelia's husband," she explained for the sake of her own husband.

"Hey there, mate," said Dante, giving Chase's hand a vigorous shake.

"And this must be your dear, sweet Gam-Gam," said Dante, eyeing Gran with a twinkle in his eye. "I've heard so much about you, Gam-Gam!"

"Well, ain't that swell," said Gran, enduring a hug from the prince.

"It's been too long, Gam-Gam," said Tessa now, giving Gran a one-armed hug while hoisting the baby higher against her chest. "How have you been?"

"Oh, can't complain," said Gran cautiously.

"And how is Gum Gum?" asked Dante. "Still a dodgy old codger, eh?"

Gran narrowed her eyes at Angela, whom she seemed to blame for this ordeal, then plastered a fake smile on her face. "Gum Gum is great. Still chasing skirts and getting hammered in bars."

Angela cleared her throat and stepped forward. "Why don't we show them their rooms? I'm sure they'll want to get freshened up before going to bed."

"Going to bed?" asked Gran. "It's nine o'clock."

"Midnight here, Gran," said Odelia. "The time

45

difference?"

"Oh, great," said Gran. "So they just stole five hours from me?"

"Nobody stole five hours."

"You're young—you don't understand. Wait till you're my age. Five hours makes a big difference."

"And these must be your lovely cats," said Tessa, eyeing me with affection.

"Yup. These are my babies," said Odelia.

"Odelia has always been a cat lover," Tessa explained for the sake of Dante. "Even when we were little she would take in strays and feed them behind her mom's back."

"That's me," said Odelia. "The stray cat lady."

"We better take them in," said Gran. "We don't want them to catch a cold."

I had to admit it was a little chilly in England, or at least a lot chillier than over in the States. Then again, this was an island, and aren't islands usually colder than the mainland? Clearly I was ill-prepared for this trip. I should have studied that travel guide more closely!

Everyone filed into the cottage and then... promptly forgot all about us!

"Um... can someone please get us out of these damn boxes!" Brutus yelled.

The car had left, and the cottage door had closed, but we were still out there.

"They forgot about us," said Harriet, summing up the situation nicely. "Can you believe that?"

"I can believe it," said Dooley, "because I'm living it."

"I have to tinkle," I announced.

"Tinkle in your box," Brutus suggested.

"I want to tinkle in my litter box."

"Newsflash, Maxie, baby. They didn't bring our litter boxes."

"What do you mean they didn't bring them? I need my litter box."

'They probably want us to tinkle in the bushes," said Dooley, glancing around. Darkness had fallen and the sounds of the night pierced the silence.

Owls were hooting, twigs were snapping, and critters were scurrying.

Just then, the front door opened and a strange-looking creature shuffled out in our direction. He looked like a dog, but I wasn't sure he was a dog. He had one of those weird faces, with the snaggleteeth and the flaps of superfluous flesh dangling all over the place. Almost as if he used to have a face at one time but it had gotten scrambled up in a cement mixer somehow.

"So you're the cats, huh?" said this strange creature.

"That's right," I said. "And what are you?"

"I'm Fluffy," the creature said gruffly.

"What are you exactly, Fluffy?" asked Harriet with a look of distaste.

"I'm a dog, of course. What did you think I was?"

"Oh, I'm not sure," she said. "Celebrities keep all kinds of weird pets these days."

The creature laughed loudly, indicating it possessed a sense of humor. "You're funny, cat!" Then the laughter stopped, and the face was wreathed in a mournful expression. "People have called me ugly. Do you think I'm ugly?"

"Of course not," I said. "You're just... special."

"If you have to know, I'm an English bulldog."

"Of course you are," I said.

"Could you do us a favor, Fluffy?" Harriet asked. "Could you go and fetch your master and tell her to get us out of these boxes and into the house?"

"Oh, sure," Fluffy said, and instantly turned on his heel—

or was it her heel?—and returned indoors. There was loud barking, and moments later Odelia came hurrying out.

"I'm so sorry, you guys!" she said. "I must have fallen asleep."

"Lamest excuse ever," Brutus growled.

"I know, right? I thought I closed my eyes for only a second but it must have been minutes. Must be that dreadful jet lag." She quickly opened the snaps on our boxes and finally we were free again!

"I have to tinkle," I announced. "Please point me to my litter box."

"You'll find everything you need inside," she said with a smile and a pat on my head. "Tessa has made arrangements for you guys and I think you'll be pleasantly surprised."

We followed her in and then into a room off the kitchen, and the moment I set paw inside I saw she hadn't lied: four litter boxes stood lined up against one wall, with a row of bowls against the other, and the scent wafting in from those big bowls told me this vacation may not have gotten off to a good start, but from here on out it was only going to get better and better. And better.

CHAPTER 9

$\mathcal{O}$delia was impressed with the cottage. When she'd heard the word cottage it had brought to mind something cute and small and romantic, but maybe also a little musty. The first image the word had elicited was the cottage Kate Winslet lived in—and Cameron Diaz moved into—in *The Holiday*, still one of her favorite holiday movies. But Tessa and Dante's home wasn't so much a cottage but a big house. There were several very spacious bedrooms, a large living space with open kitchen and a large office. The whole thing had been recently renovated, and looked more like an upscale hotel than an old cottage.

It was all very nicely done. The room she and Chase had at their disposal had a luxurious ensuite bathroom, and was itself the size of a small apartment.

Tessa explained that the cottage used to be four different units, where four different people lived. Now it had been converted back into a single-family home with space for guests and family to come and stay when they wanted to.

"This place is amazing," Odelia told Chase as she tucked a

suitcase under the bed. She'd finished unpacking and had time to admire their surroundings.

"Yeah, it definitely beats that tiny cottage Kate Winslet and Cameron Diaz house-swapped in *The holiday*," he said.

"Jinx!" she said. "I love that movie!"

"Yeah, for a chick flick it's not bad."

She slapped his shoulder and together they rolled onto the big bed. It was one of those boxspring affairs she loved so much, and the sheets were high-thread-count Egyptian cotton. "So how are we going to do this?" she asked.

"Well, obviously we're going to have to be very circumspect," he said, placing his hands behind his head. "If no one is supposed to know about what's going on here, it's going to make our work that much harder."

Chase was a cop, and for a cop things were pretty straightforward. You identify your list of suspects, you interrogate those suspects, and you try to figure out the truth. When you've selected the most likely suspect, you lean on them until they fess up and that's it. The rest is up to the legal system.

Here, Chase couldn't drag suspects into rooms with one-way mirrors. Subtlety was the name of the game, something he wasn't very adapt in.

Max came padding into the room. "This place is awesome," he announced.

"Yeah, awesome," Dooley confirmed, padding in right behind his friend.

"What are they saying?" asked Chase.

"They're saying they like it here. The exact word is 'awesome.'"

Chase grinned. "They took the words right out of my mouth. This place is like a five-star hotel, only better."

A maid tapped politely on the door. "Will there be anything else, Miss Poole?" she asked.

"No, we're good," said Odelia. Then, when the young woman made signs of retreating discreetly, she quickly added, "Or wait—maybe there's one thing."

"Yes, Miss Poole?"

The maid was young and pretty, with long auburn hair and hazel eyes. She wouldn't have looked out of place in a Richard Curtis movie, where the prime minister falls in love with his secretary, or the bestseller writer with his maid.

"Have you worked here long, Miss…"

"Suzy," said the girl. "I've been with the Duke and Duchess six months now, Ma'am," she said deferentially.

"And do you like working for my cousin?" asked Odelia, trying to keep things casual and not make it sound like an interrogation.

"Oh, yes, Miss Poole."

"Please call me Odelia," said Odelia.

"They're a wonderful couple. A breath of fresh air," said the girl, enthusiasm making her face light up. "I was with the Baroness Emilia Hartford before, and she was… quite demanding."

"More demanding than Tessa and Dante, I suppose?"

"Oh, yes," said the girl with a smile. "Very much so. The Duke and Duchess are very disciplined, with a lot going on in their lives, but they never take it out on their staff."

"Angela told me there are a lot of people that don't seem to like Tessa all that much," said Odelia, trying to inject a note of cousinly concern into her voice. "I don't suppose you've noticed any of that here, have you?"

"Oh, but everyone loves her," said the girl, eyes wide and innocent. "She's so wonderful, so elegant, so amazing in every way. The people who say bad things about her should be ashamed of themselves. They don't know her the way that I do." She clasped a hand to her face. "I didn't mean to sound so…"

"No, that's fine. I'm just worried about my cousin, that's all. And if there's anyone out there who means her harm, I think it's important to know."

"Of course."

"In America we have a lot of crackpots," Chase explained. "Nutjobs who wouldn't hesitate to take a potshot at a celebrity like Tessa. It's so great that you don't have that kind of thing going on over here."

"Oh, but we do. I've heard people say nasty things about the Duchess. Whenever I hear a comment like that I always remind them the Duke is very lucky to have her, and so are we. Before he met her, the Duke was a little bit of a wild child. A real party prince. He used to get into so much trouble." She smiled shyly. "I'm sorry. I probably shouldn't say things like that."

"Oh, no, that's fine. I think it's great that you defend them like that," said Odelia. "So the people who say these bad things, are they here in the house?"

Suzy darted a quick look behind her, then lowered her voice. "Cook says the most horrible things behind the Duchess's back."

"What kind of things?"

"Don't tell her I said this, but she told me she thinks the Duchess is entirely too arrogant for her own good and someone should teach her a lesson."

"The cook said that?"

Suzy nodded. "She thinks the Duchess doesn't appreciate her. She also says the Duke was much better off without her, and I always tell her that's a lie. The Duke has finally become a man. Before, he was just a boy. A very silly boy." She smiled "And now if you'll excuse me, I have to go check on the others."

"Of course," said Odelia. "Thanks, Suzy. And don't worry. Whatever you tell me stays between us, all right?"

Suzy gave her a quick nod and then scooted off, obviously embarrassed about the things she'd allowed herself to divulge to a total stranger.

Odelia turned to Chase. "So the cook, huh?"

"It's always the cook that did it," he said laconically. "Or is it the butler?"

CHAPTER 10

$\mathcal{D}$ooley and I were sneaking down the corridor. We were on a mission—a mission of the utmost importance. I was feeling like one of those soldiers who are tasked with the smuggling of important letters or instructions across enemy lines. Only the enemy lines in this particular place weren't that easy to pinpoint. The enemy was an unknown, and he or she could strike at any moment. I, for one, couldn't understand how Tessa could remain so calm under the circumstances. If someone was trying to kill me by dropping stones on my head and poisoning my tea I'd probably freak out and run for the hills.

But here she was, bravely staying put and facing her attacker.

We finally arrived at Tessa and Dante's room, and I saw we were in luck: the door was ajar. So we snuck inside and proceeded into the room. Like Odelia's and Chase's, this had once been the province of a single staff member, and had since been turned into spacious and comfortable lodgings for the royal couple. A connecting door led to what I assumed was the nursery, as I could hear baby noises. Tessa and Dante were in there, a TV playing in the bedroom.

The target of our mission wasn't present, though—or at least not as far as I could tell from a first cursory examination of the room. And then I saw him—or her? Fluffy was lounging in an overstuffed chair, intently watching the screen, where the news of the day was playing. An earthquake in Turkey, an oil spill in the Gulf, and war in West-Africa. Not much news on the news.

"Psst," I whispered.

"Psst," Dooley echoed.

"Hey. You. Dog."

"Fluffy!"

The English bulldog looked down and studied us with interest.

"What's up?" I asked.

"As you can see I'm working on my general education. What's up with you? And why are you whispering?"

"We wanted to have a quick word before everyone retired for the night."

"Oh, of course. What do you want to talk about? The weather? The economy? Or would you prefer some gossip hot from the gossip mill?"

"I'll have some gossip hot from the gossip mill please," said Dooley.

"Please be quiet, Dooley," I said. "Let me handle the negotiations."

"Oh, all right," Dooley said, and plunked himself down in front of the TV.

"I don't know if anybody has told you this," I began, "but Odelia is not actually a cousin of Tessa's. In fact they're no relation at all."

"Oh?" said the dog, visibly intrigued by this denouement.

"Odelia is an amateur sleuth, and Chase is a cop. They're

here to investigate an incident that took place when a rock almost fell on top of Tessa."

"By the way," said Dooley. "Are you a boy or a girl, Fluffy?"

"A girl, of course. Can't you tell?"

Dooley shook his head. "Not really."

Subtlety has never been Dooley's strong suit.

"Anyway," I said, trying to get the conversation back on track. "So about that incident with the ball of stone dropping down from a great height…"

Fluffy shivered. "Oh, I was there. It was horrible. Absolutely ghastly."

"I can only imagine. And the tea incident? Were you there for that as well?"

She nodded slowly. "How do you know about all this?"

"We have our sources," said Dooley. "And I'm afraid they're classified."

"No, they're not," I said, hoping Dooley would stop sabotaging the investigation. "Our source is Angela. She and Tessa are trying to figure out what's going on."

"What's going on is that someone is trying to murder my human, cat."

"You can call me Max."

"And I'm Dooley," said Dooley, in case Fluffy hadn't caught on.

"So… if your human is an amateur sleuth, does that make you cat sleuths?"

"That's classified," said Dooley.

"No, it's not. Yes, we are cat sleuths. We help Odelia solve murders and other crimes. By going where no human has gone before."

"Mars?"

"Places where humans don't usually go, like back alleys,

and the nooks and crannies where only strange creatures stir." And strange dogs.

"You make it sound so exciting," said Fluffy.

"Well, it is. And dangerous, of course," I said. "You wouldn't believe how many dangers my fellow cats and I have braved to help our dear human."

Okay, so maybe I was laying it on a bit thick, but I like to think I was doing it in service of my mission: to get this mutt's full participation.

"So what do you want me to do?" Fluffy asked.

"I want you to think hard and tell me who might be behind these attacks."

She thought hard, judging from the wrinkles on her face —well, more wrinkles than usual, I mean.

"The stone," I said when nothing seemed forthcoming. "Think back to that stone dropping. Did you see anyone on the roof? Pushing that stone down?"

She shook her head, eyes squeezed tightly shut now. "I only had eyes for my human, and that horrible stone that nearly crushed her to death."

"So you didn't look up?"

She shook her head again.

"What about the tea?"

"What about the tea?"

"Do you like tea?" asked Dooley.

"Not particularly, no," said the dog.

"Oh. I thought, you being English and all, you'd love tea."

"Dooley," I said warningly.

"Just establishing Fluffy's frame of mind," said Dooley.

I tamped down a groan. "Tessa was given a cup of tea laced with Belladonna. Do you have any idea who might have poured her that tea?"

"Cook," Fluffy said instantly. "That's the only person I can think of."

Now we were getting somewhere.

"Who brought her the tea?"

"Suzy. The maid."

"She could have dumped that poison in."

"She seems like a nice person, this Suzy," Dooley commented. "Just saying," he added when I gave him a censorious look.

"She is nice," Fluffy agreed. "Which is why she would never poison Tessa's tea. Suzy is devoted to Tessa."

"See?" said Dooley. "She has a nice face. Not the face of a killer."

"And how would you know what a killer's face looks like?" I asked.

"Killers are mean—they have mean faces. Suzy has a nice face."

There was no arguing with Dooley, so I decided to ignore him. "What about this cook person?" I asked.

"Yes, well. Cook doesn't like Tessa. Never has. Whenever I'm in the kitchen prancing around all she does is complain about Tessa. On and on it goes. Quite galling. Not at all pleasant to hear someone badmouth your human like that."

"What does she say?"

"That Tessa is arrogant, thinks she knows best, always interferes with her work—Cook's work, I mean. Tessa has very particular ideas about the food she eats. What she considers healthy choices. So she gives precise instructions what to cook for her and Dante. In fact she's in the kitchen all the time, trying out new recipes, using the blender to make green smoothies for herself and her husband, experimenting with different ingredients and recipes."

"And Cook doesn't like that."

"Oh, she hates it. Says she's never worked for anyone as prissy and utterly demanding as Tessa, which I'm sure is simply not true."

"Do you think she hates her enough to try and murder her?"

Fluffy thought hard again, screwing up her face so much her nose disappeared between her eyebrows, then reemerged when she opened her mouth to speak. "I'm not sure," she said finally. "I've seen my fair share of Sherlock Holmes on TV, and even Father Brown. But it's hard to determine who the killer is, if you can't actually see them do it, if you see what I mean."

"Those TV detectives are all very clever," I agreed. "In real life it's a lot harder to figure out whodunit."

"Exactly. They make it look so easy."

"They do make it look easy," said Dooley. "Like Aurora Teagarden. I like Aurora Teagarden," he explained. "She's a librarian and she's very pretty."

Fluffy and I waited for him to tell us more about Aurora Teagarden and why he liked her so much but this seemed to be the extent of his remarks on the subject. So I thanked Fluffy, figuring I'd elicited all the information I could expect, and would have retreated back to the safety of Odelia's room if Dante hadn't waltzed in from the nursery and closed the door, cutting off our line of retreat!

"I can't believe this!" he was shouting. "You do this every time!"

"Keep your voice down! You'll wake up Silvy!" Tessa hissed.

Oh, heck. We'd just landed ourselves in the middle of a domestic dispute!

CHAPTER 11

*D*ooley and I had crawled under the sofa, not wanting to be seen trespassing, and had a worm's-eye view of both Fluffy and the quarreling couple. Fluffy, who seemed to have resigned herself to the quarrel, watched the news, from time to time darting an anxious look at her owners, then down to us, as if to say: 'Can you believe this?'

I could—even though I didn't want to!

"Oh, this is rich," said Dante once Tessa had closed to the door to the nursery. "First you tell me I can't go to the pub and now you're telling me I can't even invite a mate over for a quiet drink? You're too much, Tessa."

"You know as well as I do that it won't be quiet for very long when Damien drops by."

"I never see the bloke anymore!"

"You told me yourself you needed to grow up. That things were different now that Silvy is in our lives. That Damien doesn't fit with the Dante you want to be."

"He's been my best mate since we were kids!"

"So go and see him! But not at the pub. You know what people will say."

"People talk regardless of what I do. So do I have to stay cooped up in here for the rest of my life? I didn't sign up to be a recluse, Tessa. I'm too young to turn into one of those long-bearded blokes who shuffle around in their PJs with crumbs caked to their face and hair growing out of every orifice."

Tessa stared at him for a moment, then couldn't keep a straight face and neither could he. They both burst out laughing, and soon were wiping away tears.

"Are they crying now?" asked Dooley.

"They're tears of laughter," I explained.

"I don't get it. Can you laugh and cry at the same time?"

"Humans can. They laugh so hard they get teary-eyed. It's true," I added when he gave me a skeptical look.

"It's true," Fluffy said from the couch. "Humans are weird."

That, they definitely were.

"I'm sorry," said Dante. "But the beard thing could actually happen."

"I know, right!" said Tessa. "It could happen to me, too. You'd have a bearded lady for a wife."

"I like to think I'd love you even if you did grow a beard," he said, taking her into his arms.

She put up a token resistance, then said, grinning, "I think I'd rather fancy you with a beard."

"One of them long and tangled ones?"

"With the crumbs tacked to your face."

"Oh, puh-lease," said Fluffy, but to Dante and Tessa it must have sounded like a bark, for they both looked up and laughed.

"See?" said Tessa. "Even Fluffy thinks you should grow a beard."

"Oh, no, I don't," said Fluffy. "I hate bearded blokes. So tickly."

"Maybe I will," said Dante.

"Please don't!" said Fluffy.

"Is that a threat or a promise?" asked Tessa.

"I meant it as a threat, actually."

"To me it sounded like a promise."

Kissing ensued, as it invariably does in these types of situations, and Dooley and I turned away, as did Fluffy. Us pets aren't into mushiness.

"Dante doesn't look like a man trying to murder his wife," said Dooley, and for once I had to admit he'd hit the nail on the head. Unless Dante was a great actor, he genuinely appeared to love his wife.

"I think we can remove Dante from our list of suspects," I said.

From the next room, crying could be heard, and both parents hurried over.

We could have used this as our chance to escape, if only the door hadn't been closed shut. And from where we sat, I didn't see any other means of escape, either.

"Psst," said Fluffy suddenly.

"We're stuck here!" I told her.

"I know! I have an idea!"

She then started barking loudly, jumped down from the couch and moved to the door. The barking intensified, and was now accompanied by a frenzied scratching of the door.

"All right, all right," said Dante, as he came running. "Gotta go, sweetie?"

"Yes, please," said Fluffy.

Dante grabbed a leash from the credenza, hooked it into Fluffy's collar, and opened the door.

Fluffy turned to us and winked, indicating this was our chance!

So we took it. Moving like the wind—or at least two cats

intent on escaping—we were through that door and out into the living area like a flash!

"Thanks, Fluffy!" I yelled over my shoulder.

"Yes, thank you so much, Fluffy!" Dooley chimed in.

"You're welcome!" the dog yelled back.

"Was that... a cat?" I could hear Dante ask.

To which Fluffy replied, "I didn't see nothing."

And we were going well and moving in the direction of Odelia's room when suddenly I collided heavily with an immovable object. The immovable object turned out to be a large lady, who suddenly bent down and picked me up by the front legs, so that the rest of my not inconsiderable corpus was left dangling. Not a pleasant position to be in, let me assure you!

"And what do we have here?" she asked sternly. I was face to face with the woman now, and I was reminded of Dante's joke about growing a long and tangled beard. This woman did have a beard, and a mustache, too. Neither of them was particularly long or tangled but they were still there. "Out with you lot," she grumbled, and hoisted me in the direction of the door.

"Hey, no!" I said. "I'm an honored guest here."

"Max?" said Dooley. "Where is that woman taking you?"

Of course she didn't understand me. She was one of those people who seem to think that cats belong out on the street and have no business being inside the house.

So she opened the door and threw me out. Actually threw me out! Then she returned to grab Dooley by the scruff of the neck and repeated the procedure. Quick as a flash, I tried to return indoors, but she blocked my passage, snapping, "Cats don't belong in the house. Now bugger off."

And then she slammed the door in our faces!

CHAPTER 12

*T*here was a tap at the door and Odelia went to open it. She was surprised to find none other than Tessa standing before her. "Can I come in?" she asked.

The newly-minted royal looked anxious, Odelia thought, and nervous.

"Of course," said Odelia. "This is your house."

Tessa nodded and quickly closed the door behind her. "So?" she asked. "Any news?"

Chase, who'd been channel-surfing and had finally decided to watch sports on ITV, walked over. "Hey, cousin," he said.

Tessa grimaced. She clearly was not in the mood for levity. "I'm sorry, but I'm so nervous I can't think straight. My heart is beating a mile a minute, like, all the time. And the worst part? That I have to lie to Dante about all this."

"Your mother seems to feel very strongly about him," said Odelia.

"She does. I've told her already that Dante can't be behind this—he just can't—but she doesn't believe me. She feels that it's better not to tell him anything. And it's killing me!"

"I can only imagine," said Odelia. If she suspected Chase of wanting to kill her she'd probably feel exactly the way Tessa did right now.

"So who are your suspects?"

"Well, we have the list your mother gave us," said Odelia, handing Tessa the list. "Your cousin Nesbit drew it up."

Tessa stifled a shocked cry. "This is every single person I've been in contact with. My cook, housekeeper, maid, assistant, Dante... Wait, what is the Queen doing on this list?"

"That was Angela's addition. She feels the Queen doesn't like you all that much, and might have gotten it into her nut to have you bumped off. Her words, not mine."

"She thinks the Queen wants to make your death look like an accident," said Chase.

Tessa shook her head. "I don't believe this. The Queen has been nothing but kind to me. I can't believe she'd want to have me crushed or poisoned."

"Who's Damien Card?" asked Odelia, indicating suspect number five.

"Dante's oldest friend. I guess the logic is that Damien thinks I stole Dante from him. And in a sense that's true. Ever since we got married Dante hasn't spent as much time with his old chums as he used to. But that's not my fault. That's because Dante has been busy with other stuff. Like becoming a father for the first time. And it's a little weird for a father to drink himself into a coma or to get arrested for stealing a constable's helmet and tie it to a church spire."

Odelia gave the Duchess a questioning look. "Boys will be boys?"

"Apparently that's the kind of stuff Dante was up to before we met. Before he turned into a responsible husband and father."

"Which is why Damien is upset with you," Chase said.

"I guess. But it's hardly a reason to try and kill me.

Though I suppose it could be true. Damien is a spoiled rich kid. Very immature and peevish."

"I talked to Suzy," said Odelia. "She said Cook speaks very harshly of you. Doesn't like you meddling with her cooking."

Tessa nodded. "I know. She hates it. I'd fire her and do everything myself—it would spare me the aggravation of having to deal with her grumpiness and her constant badgering. Unfortunately I just don't have the time."

"You could always hire another cook," Chase suggested. "One that doesn't try to kill you."

Tessa smiled. "Carolyn may not like me very much, but I hardly think that's a reason to kill me."

"She did make the tea that was poisoned," Odelia reminded her.

"And Suzy brought me that tea," said Tessa. "After it had been standing on the kitchen counter for God knows how long. It was almost cold by the time I got it."

"Which means anyone with access to the kitchen could have dumped in the Belladonna," said Odelia.

"We need to talk to this Carolyn person," said Chase.

"Oh, this is all so frustrating," Tessa groaned with an irritated shrug. "If only we could have this out in the open, so the police could come in and properly question everyone. Look for potential witnesses. That sort of thing."

"Why don't you?" asked Odelia.

Tessa threw up her arms. "Mom's idea, and she does have a point. There's this *thing* going on in the media right now. A regular shit storm. And I'm right in the middle of it. They invent story after story, making me look like evil incarnate. They'd probably claim I invented this whole murder story just so I could get attention. It would be amazingly awkward and embarrassing to the royal family, and put Dante in a really tough spot." She shook her head. "No, we need to be very discreet about this. Nothing can leak to the media or the

Queen will kick me out of the family for good, royal baby or not."

"So the cook, the maid, the best friend... How about your housekeeper? Does she have a reason to want to get rid of you?"

"I suppose," said Tessa. "She claims I stick my nose where it doesn't belong. But it's my household, after all, and I have very particular ideas about what I want and don't want."

"And so does she."

"So does she," Tessa confirmed. "Which means we don't always see eye to eye."

"And what does Dante think about all of this?"

"He doesn't get involved. He's actually used to this sort of thing. His mom had very particular ideas, too, and so does his grandmother, obviously. He'll always back me up, but he doesn't want to come across all heavy-handed either. He likes to keep the peace, and hates to make a big fuss over things."

"Tough spot to be in, for you," said Odelia.

"You have no idea," said Tessa, crinkling her brow. "It's been a tough couple of months. Everything I say is misinterpreted, whatever I do is wrong, and wherever I go I'm gawked at as if I'm some kind of circus freak."

"At least the people still support you. Angela says you're popular."

"Yes, but for how long? Their minds are poisoned and they're being set up against me. And who are they going to believe? The media that writes garbage about me every single day, or me, who can't say a word in my own defense? Dante says I shouldn't take it personally. He says it's a kind of hazing thing the English press do with every single person who marries into The Firm."

"The what?"

She smiled. "The royal family, also known as The Firm."

She sighed. "I'm not so sure, though. I talked to Dante's aunt the other day, and she says she's never seen it being played so rough and so vicious. She thinks it might have something to do with the fact that I'm not English born."

"Or the fact that you're a charming, intelligent, attractive and outspoken young woman," said Chase, which earned him a laugh from Tessa and a smile from Odelia.

"Thanks," said Tessa. "It's nice to know that there are still some people in the world who don't think I'm the worst thing to happen to this country."

"Let's focus on finding the person trying to kill you," said Odelia. "Speaking of which, what do your protection people say?"

"Well, my cousin says it must be someone with access to my schedule, so presumably someone in my inner circle. For instance the fact that I was going to be at the Newtmore Summer Show at that exact time."

"Who would have known about that?"

Tessa held up the list. "Everyone on this list, and the people on my protection detail, of course."

"Could they be behind this?"

"Oh, I don't think so. My cousin vouches for them. They've all worked for the royal family for so long—they're really devoted."

"That could be the reason they're doing this."

"If they see me as a threat to the monarchy, you mean."

"Exactly."

Tessa blinked. "If that's the case, then this list isn't nearly long enough. There are probably thousands of people who wish me harm right now—maybe millions."

CHAPTER 13

I didn't mind being locked out. What I did mind was being locked out in an environment that was basically unknown to me. No familiar faces here, or even familiar sounds of the night. No, it was all very new and frankly a little scary. So I did what any sensible cat would do: I cleared my throat and politely asked, "Um, could anyone please let us in?"

"Yes, please," echoed Dooley. "I would like to go to bed now."

When that didn't seem to yield immediate results, we tried a different tack: we both started yowling—loudly! Unfortunately Baby Silvy chose this exact moment to start yowling, too. And as much as it pains me to admit it: she beat us squarely in the yowling department. Apparently we have much to learn, and Silvy was leading the way. So our yowling was drowned out by the noise of the royal baby, and we had to pursue other avenues to resolve our situation.

We checked the house for a possible means of egress. And that's when I saw it—or, rather, him. A man was sitting in a car, parked nearby, with one of those very large cameras obscuring a large part of his face, shooting pictures of the house. I could hear the shutter going clickety-click as he did.

"Who's that, Max?" asked Dooley.

"That's a paparazzo, Dooley."

"What's a paparazzo?"

"It's a kind of parasite. It breeds on other humans, sucking their lifeblood."

"Nasty things.

"Very nasty," I agreed.

"Is he taking our picture, you think?"

I darted a quick look at the house, and realized he wasn't. Through the window, Tessa's profile was outlined. She was holding Silvy, consoling her.

"Bad paparazzo," said Dooley, who'd noticed the same thing.

"Very bad indeed," I said. Taking snapshots of a private scene for the sole purpose of exploiting it for monetary gain.

And Prince Dante must have had the exact same thought, for at that moment he returned from his walk with Fluffy and spotted the man sitting in front of his cottage.

"Hey!" he bellowed. "What the hell do you think you're doing?"

The man, caught, instantly started up his engine. In response, Fluffy started yapping like a mad dog, and then, before Dante could stop her, launched herself through the open window of the car and onto the paparazzo, who was making frantic efforts of putting his car in gear and driving away.

The man yelped in dismay as the thirty-pound English bulldog landed in his lap, and the next moment the car lurched forward, the dog still inside, with Dante running after it, yelling and screaming all the while for the car to stop.

It was pandemonium out there, and just as I wondered

what had happened to all the security people who were supposedly guarding the royal couple, a burly man came running out of the house, still clutching a sandwich, took one look at the Prince, racing after the car, and went in pursuit, sticking a finger of his free hand into his ear for some reason and yelling to himself.

Instantly, three more men came running out of the house, and now the gag was complete: the paparazzo was obviously in the lead, with Dante right on his heels, and four security people chasing after him. It would have been funny if it hadn't been so serious, and I really felt for Fluffy, being abducted like this without a moment's notice.

I would have run after the group, if I had the kind of body made for exertion. As it is, I'm more of an intellectual than an action hero. Dooley obviously felt the same way, for he stayed put right next to me.

The door flew open once more, and disgorged even more people: Tessa, cradling the baby, Odelia, Chase, Angela, and some of the household staff, who apparently worked long hours. All of them started running in the same direction the others had gone, except for Tessa, who had the baby to contend with. Harriet and Brutus were the next ones to emerge from the house, and joined us in staring after the strange nocturnal fitness activity.

"What's going on?" asked Brutus.

"A paparazzo was taking pictures of Tessa, and when Dante saw it, he decided to put a stop to it. Oh, and Fluffy jumped into the car and the paparazzi drove off with her, so there's that to take into consideration."

"Terrible business," said Brutus. "Do you think the paparazzo is the one who tried to kill Tessa?"

"I doubt it. You can't kill a person by taking their picture."

"There are some people who believe that you can," said Harriet. "They believe that by taking your picture, they control you. That's why some people never want their picture taken, so no one can do them any harm."

Dooley shivered. "Creepy," he said. "Imagine someone takes your picture and decides to do all sorts of bad things with it. I don't think I'd like that."

"I don't understand how he was allowed to get this close to the house," said Brutus. "Aren't they supposed to have a security perimeter?"

"I guess royal security isn't all it's cracked up to be," I said.

"Or maybe the English are more loosey-goosey when it comes to security."

From the house, Gran now emerged. "What's going on?" she asked.

I repeated my brief summary of recent events, and she tsk-tsked freely.

"Bad business," she said. "If those damn paps can get this close to the house, anyone can." She pushed at her white curls, which were a little lopsided. She'd obviously been sleeping when the ruckus erupted.

"Do you think that a person can gain control over you by taking your picture, Gran?" asked Dooley. He seemed worried now, after learning about this new and hitherto unknown-to-him potential threat.

"No, I don't," said Gran. "If that were the case, all the politicians, celebrities, and people in the public eye would be under the control of the millions of people who look at their pictures. Heck, I had a picture of Rock Hudson on my wall for ages, hoping one day he'd happen to be in town and swing by. Do you think he ever did? Nah, don't you believe that crap."

"It's like voodoo," Harriet insisted. "Where they put a pin in a little doll?"

"Rubbish," said Gran decidedly.

She seemed to know what she was talking about, almost

as if she'd had her likeness turned into a doll and had strange people put pins in them all her life.

Just then, the paparazzo's car came driving back up the road, only this time with Prince Dante behind the wheel. A long procession followed, including but not limited to Chase, Odelia, four security people, and... the pap, hands tied in front of him with plastic handcuffs. Waddling behind them was Fluffy, who looked particularly pleased with herself. She had a piece of cloth clasped between her teeth, which was an exact match for the hole in the pap's pants.

It was a great night for a good dog.

CHAPTER 14

"*I* have every right to be here," said the man, looking particularly cross that Fluffy had bitten him in the ass. "And you have no right to detain me—or to confiscate my camera and destroy the images I shot!"

The security people had parked the man's car, and were now taking a crack at the paparazzo. The police had been called, and they'd be there soon.

"Who is he?" asked Odelia as she found herself standing next to Tessa and her mother.

"Otis Robins. He's a famous reporter," said Tessa. "He has his own show on television and everything, and he writes for one of the big tabloids."

"So what was he doing out here, taking pictures of you?"

"He says his regular photographer bailed on him so he decided to take his place. He's doing a series of articles on me and this appears to be part of it."

"Major-league jerk, if you ask me," said Angela, who glowered at the man.

"Yeah, he's leading the charge against me," said Tessa. "Must hate me something pretty bad."

"So what did you ever do to him that makes him hate you so much?" asked Odelia.

"Beats me. I never met the man before in my life."

"You married a prince," said Angela. "These islanders always react viciously when an outsider moves in and sweeps up one of their own."

"Or maybe his daughter had a crush on Dante and really wanted to marry him," Odelia suggested.

"From the way he's acting, you could very well be right," said Tessa.

The reporter and Dante stood toe to toe, with the Duke shouting that the man was out of line and would pay dearly for this breach of privacy.

"Who cares a sod about your privacy?!" Otis Robbins yelled, his face red and the veins at his temples throbbing furiously. "You're a public person—you have no privacy!"

"See?" said Tessa. "This is what I have to deal with. And all because I happened to fall in love with a sweet and gentle guy."

"Tough," said Odelia as she watched the reporter closely. "So could he be the one trying to kill you?"

"Who knows?" said Tessa. "I'm starting to think they're all out to get me."

"At least you have your security people," said Angela, squeezing her daughter's arm. "I think they'll be more vigilant from now on."

"I hope so. They haven't exactly done a great job so far."

"Maybe you should talk to the police," Odelia suggested. "Tell them about the stone thing, and the poisoned tea. They have resources we don't. And they can protect you and put the word out. The killer will probably think twice before trying again if he or she knows that the police are onto them."

"Out of the question," said Angela. "Tess's position is iffy as it is. If the public became aware there's a killer out to get her, there will be a big scandal. The Queen will personally kick her out of the family and the country."

"Dante would never allow that," said Odelia.

"Dante would have to choose between staying married to my daughter or having a place in the royal family."

"The Queen would never do that."

"Oh, yes, she would. There's a precedent. The Queen's uncle married an American widow and was forced to abdicate and was pretty much ostracized."

"That was a long time ago," said Odelia. "The times have changed."

"I wouldn't be so sure. A murder scandal? That's the last thing this family needs. No, this has to stay under wraps. It absolutely must. Right, Tessa?"

Tessa nodded distractedly. She was pale, Odelia thought, the whole thing clearly getting under the young woman's skin. Which wasn't surprising.

"Okay, fine," she said. "Chase and I will figure it out." And the cats, she thought. Though so far they didn't have a lot to go on. Then again, they'd only been there for a couple of hours.

"Tomorrow I have an important speech I need to give in town," said Tessa. "Will you join me? It would mean a lot if you did. And you, of course, Mom."

"We will be there," said Odelia.

"Of course, honey," said Angela. "I won't leave your side for a second."

"Thanks—and sorry about all of this. When I got married to Dante I never dreamed..." She stifled a muted sob.

"Oh, honey," said Angela, rubbing her daughter's back. "You couldn't have known things would get so bad."

Tessa nodded, and the three women stared at the reporter, who was still defending his constitutional right to take pictures of a royal, for his own benefit and that of his bank account.

Despicable man, Odelia thought. How could he live with himself? He didn't look like a murderer, though. But when she thought that camera he aimed at Tessa and the baby could very well have been a gun, she shivered.

"You really need to talk to your cousin," she said. "This should never have been allowed to happen."

"I will," said Tessa. "For the sake of Silvy, this absolutely can't happen again."

As if she understood, Silvy sneezed, and the three women smiled. At least there was one little ray of sunshine in Tessa's life.

CHAPTER 15

$\mathcal{T}$he house was quiet and not a creature stirred except for four cats and, possibly, one dog. Though I imagined Fluffy was sleeping contentedly, that swath of fabric she'd ripped from the reporter's pants between her paws.

Odelia had left the door to the room open, so we could come and go as we pleased. She would have done the same with the window that led out to a wraparound terrace but that wouldn't have been wise. Besides, all the windows had security locks on them, and they were all connected to the security system that fed into the security room at the back of the house, where activity had been ramped up after the disastrous incident with the reporter.

Odelia and Chase were watching an interview with that very same reporter, where the man railed virulently against Tessa and demanded she 'fall in line or bugger the hell off,' which apparently meant she had to go away.

"British English is such a strange language," Dooley commented. "Bugger the hell off. That sounds so weird and so funny at the same time."

"It does," I agreed. "But I don't think he meant it to sound funny."

Otis Robbins also claimed Tessa was the worst thing that had ever happened to England in its long history. He claimed she was up there with Adolf Hitler and the bubonic plague. It all seemed a little over the top to me. How could a sweet American girl be worse than Adolf Hitler or the bubonic plague? It only proved to me that the British tabloid press was cuckoo.

Odelia had explained there were essentially two types of media in this country. One was the quality press, who adhered to journalistic integrity, and the other the tabloid press, who just wrote whatever, whether true or false, and seemed to have it in for Tessa, whom they liked to accuse of every evil under the sun, as if she was the worst criminal ever to set foot on English soil.

"Poor Tessa," said Harriet now. "To have an entire section of the population pitted against her. Do you think she'll be able to survive out here?"

"I don't know," I admitted. "These tabloids are apparently read by millions of Britons, so they're turning her into a target for all of those readers."

"I doubt whether every single reader who picks up a so-called tabloid believes every word they write, though," said Harriet, sensibly.

"Even if only a fraction of them do, Tessa has a serious problem."

"I think she needs to move back to the States," said Brutus. "It's obvious they don't appreciate her here, so why stick it out? That's just crazy."

"I agree," said Harriet. "She should move back to the States and enjoy a wonderful life with her new husband and their newborn baby."

"But she can't," I said. "Dante has a lot of royal duties here."

"Like what?" asked Dooley.

"Like... I don't know. Probably he has to cut a lot of ribbons and open a lot of county fairs and stuff like that."

"I don't think he's going to miss cutting ribbons," said Brutus. "And if he does, there's plenty of ribbons for him to cut in the States."

"Yes," said Dooley. "There are lots of nice ribbons in Hampton Cove. He can come and live next door and cut ribbons to his heart's content."

"It's not just the ribbons, you guys," I said. "He probably has a lot of other duties, and besides, he's going to miss his family, isn't he?"

"He can Skype," said Harriet.

"Yes, he can Skype," agreed Dooley.

Speaking of Skype, just then we heard a familiar voice. It was Marge.

"Hey, honey," said Marge. "How's the jet lag?"

"Not too bad," said Odelia. "What time is it over there anyway?"

"Around dinner time."

"Yes, we were just going to start dinner," said Tex. "What time do you have?"

"Middle of the night," said Odelia. "We had a big scare just now, and we're all a little shook up."

"An intruder tried to snap pictures of Tessa and the baby," Chase said.

"How horrible," said Marge. "I hope the police arrested him?"

"No, they haven't," said Chase. "Apparently he had every right to shoot pictures, and there's not a damn thing we can do about it."

"You need to watch out, honey," said Tex. "I just read a

story about how the English hate us Yankees so much they'll do anything to get rid of us."

"I'm sure it's not as bad as all that," said Chase with a laugh.

"They don't like Tessa, though," said Marge.

"I think a lot of people love Tessa," said Odelia. "Only the tabloids don't. Unfortunately they have the biggest megaphone, which distorts the picture."

Gran had snuck into the room and sat down next to Odelia and Chase.

"Hey, honey," she said, adding after a long pause, "and Tex."

"How do you like England so far, Ma?" asked Marge.

Gran pulled a face, which said it all.

"I think she's suffering from jet lag," said Odelia.

She was right. Gran had been unusually quiet and had stayed out of trouble all night. She looked tired, too. Not her vivacious and sprightly self.

"I'm pretty much beat," she said now, confirming our suspicions.

"Better go to bed," said Odelia.

"That's the problem. I went to bed, and I can't sleep." She got up. "Maybe I need some warm milk." And she tottered off, closing the door behind her.

"Sounds like you've got your work cut out for you," said Tex. "Be careful, will you? Don't get in the line of fire."

"It's not as bad as all that," said Odelia. "It's not as if snipers are shooting at us from all sides."

"There was an incident with poisoned tea, though," said Chase.

"Poisoned tea!" Marge cried. "Oh, honey…"

"It's fine, Mom. We've got everything under control here. And as soon as we have a chance, we'll talk to some more people and figure this thing out."

"Too bad there are no more canine witnesses," said Harriet. "Or we could have solved this case already."

She was right. There was only Fluffy, and she'd already told us everything she knew.

"I have a feeling this is not going be the open-and-shut case Odelia thought it was going to be," said Dooley, and never had truer words been spoken.

Odelia and Chase said their goodbyes to her folks and logged off, then went to bed.

Soon the house was quiet, except for four cats and presumably one dog.

And I know many of you are not familiar with the concept of a watchcat, but that's how I now saw myself. After the stone incident, the tea incident, and now the reporter scare, I vowed to keep a watchful eye for potential nocturnal intruders, friendly or otherwise. And so the four of us tiptoed into the living area and took up position on the several windows that looked out into the night. I took this vigil seriously, and so did the others. I'd grown fond of Tessa, in spite of the fact that we'd only just met. A young mother with a newborn, being bullied the way she was, had touched my heart. I vowed not to let anything happen to her, even if I had to take a bite out of some human's seat of the pants myself—no matter how horrible the taste.

Soon Fluffy joined us, and we were on full animal alert.

"Let's see who dares to mess with us now," growled Brutus from the second window.

"He's going to have to get past me first," said Harriet from the third window.

"And me," said Dooley, from the fourth window.

"You know what?" said Fluffy. "I like you guys. For a bunch of cats you're all right."

Cats and dogs? Living together in peace and harmony. Who knew?!

CHAPTER 16

*I*n spite of the fact that she was bone tired, Odelia hadn't slept well. She'd been tossing and turning and kept dreaming of nocturnal intruders out to get her. So when she suddenly awoke, thinking it was still the middle of the night, she was surprised to find the sun hoisting itself cheerfully across the horizon and announcing a brand-new day.

It didn't feel like morning to her, though, and then she realized that her biological clock was still on New York time, where it was the middle of the night right now.

Chase was zonked out next to her, sleeping the sleep of the innocent, and of her four cats there was no trace.

She rubbed her eyes and glanced around at her surroundings. She was starting to realize this was a crazy mission, and maybe they'd been rash to accept it. It could literally take weeks before they figured out who was behind these attacks on Tessa, or maybe never. And all the while she was out here in London while she could have written a ton of articles for the *Hampton Cove Gazette.*

She'd promised her editor a killer article from the

London trenches, and the prospect of a couple of juicy stories about British royalty had smoothed over any objections Dan had. Still, she couldn't afford to stay away for too long, and she already felt she was imposing on Tessa's and Dante's hospitality simply by being here and sleeping under their roof.

She got up and padded barefoot to the window. Right outside, a burly security guard stood sentinel. She was pleasantly surprised. With this level of security the would-be assassin surely would think twice before trying again.

Yawning, she opened the door and walked into the living room. She was gratified to find four cats and a dog sleeping soundly on the couch. She smiled as she studied them for a moment, then went back into her room, got out her phone and returned to snap a shot of the sleeping pets. They looked so peaceful. At least the fear she had about dragging them all the way out here had been unfounded: clearly they were neither traumatized nor unhappy.

It was then that she heard voices. She decided to have a closer listen, as the voices were rising in pitch and volume. An argument was clearly brewing.

"I told you, Tessa. I can make a perfectly acceptable smoothie. In fact I wrote the book on smoothies."

"I know you did, Carolyn, But it's just something I like to do myself, so please don't take this as a comment on your work, but—"

"That's exactly what I'm doing. If you won't let me make you breakfast, lunch and dinner what did you hire me for?"

Odelia walked in to see a red-faced woman with gray hair standing, fists planted on wide hips, trying to stare Tessa down. Tessa wasn't having it, though. She was standing her ground.

"Look, I've been making my own smoothies all my life," she said, "and I'm not about to stop now just because we happen to have a wonderful cook. No offense, but if I choose to make a smoothie in my own kitchen, I'm perfectly entitled to, am I right?"

The cook, who'd noticed Odelia, shook her head disgustedly, then removed her apron, threw it on top of the kitchen counter and walked out. Obviously she wasn't happy with Tessa's smoothie-making prowess.

Tessa gave Odelia an overwrought look and Odelia returned the look with a 'What are you gonna do?' gesture. She decided to have a little chat with the cook. Strike the iron while it was hot, so to speak.

"Hey, Carolyn," she said, following the cook into the living room. "I'm sorry but I happened to overhear you and Tessa just now."

"You heard? Oh, good," said the woman, shaking her head. "Of all the overbearing…"

"You don't appreciate it when people set foot in your kitchen, is that it?" asked Odelia, who'd never had a cook before, and had no idea how the whole cook-employer dynamic worked.

"It's not that. She can make all the smoothies she wants. It's just that whatever I do, it never seems to be good enough. I made them a perfectly fine smoothie yesterday. Dante drank it and said it was the best smoothie he'd ever tasted. Tessa? She pulled a face. And then started grilling me on what I put into it. I wrote the book on smoothies! Literally. It was a bestseller. I've worked for some of the most demanding employers imaginable but she," she said, pointing a quivering finger in the direction of the kitchen, "takes the cake."

"Tough employer, huh?" said Odelia sympathetically.

"She's impossible to please! Always some point of criticism. I've had it up to here," she said, indicating her nose. "And you know what? I quit. That's right. I quit right now!"

She seemed to have just come to this conclusion. "So you tell the Duchess that she's lost her cook and good riddance!"

And with these words, she walked out before Odelia could ask her about the poisoned tea, which had been her intention in the first place.

She stared after the woman, and wondered if she was watching a killer walk away. Somehow she had a feeling she wasn't.

CHAPTER 17

*G*ran felt as if she awoke from a deep coma. "Man, oh, man," she groaned as she dragged open her eyelids. She wanted to sleep more—a lot more. But the sun was up and so should she. She was of a generation that believed in going to bed with the chickens and getting up when the cock crowed and she wasn't going to change now. She felt weary, though, and realized this was the dreaded jet lag. But she wasn't the person to let a silly little notion like that get her down. So she got up and stared at the person in the other bed.

"What are you staring at?" this person asked, and stretched awkwardly.

Memory returned and she realized who her roommate was.

"Angela," she said.

"That's my name—don't wear it out."

"Oh, God, I feel terrible," said Gran.

"Jet lag," said her roommate. "You'll get used to it."

"That's right. You've been coming and going a lot, haven't you?"

"I have. And I hate it. Each time I feel like I'm going to die."

"Must be tough," Gran offered sympathetically.

"It is. But what are you gonna do? If your only child marries a British prince, traveling to and fro kinda comes with the territory."

"Why don't you move here?"

"Are you nuts?" She gave her a critical look. "I have my own life thank you very much. I can't just uproot it just to come and be a full-time babysitter. Besides, my friends, my family, everyone and everything is back home."

"Yeah, I wouldn't want to move here either, even if Odelia married a prince."

"It's not just that. I don't want to be in their way. A young married couple doesn't need an overbearing mother hen hanging around. If I overstayed my welcome something tells me Dante would probably take a crack at me!"

"You still think it's Dante that's behind this whole terrible business?"

"I don't know what to think. Keep an open mind, right? Don't trust anyone. So why should I make an exception for the man my daughter married?"

"He seems like a great guy. The way he came to her defense last night."

"He is. And I think Tessa did very well for herself. I like the dude. He's funny, he's smart, he's handsome…"

"The perfect son-in-law!"

Angela laughed. "Exactly! Only we're too old to let appearances fool us, aren't we? And we know sometimes things are simply too good to be true."

Gran nodded. She knew better than anyone. Back home in Hampton Cove she'd helped her granddaughter solve more than one crime, and the killers sometimes turned out to be the last person she'd expected. It had shaken her belief in the essential goodness of man profoundly. Then again, she also trusted her own intuition, and her gut told her Dante was all right. Besides, what kind of man would kill his bride and mother of his newborn baby? Only a demented psychopath, and the young prince didn't strike her as one.

"Let's see what your granddaughter comes up with," said Angela. "I have faith in her. She's a good little detective."

"True," said Gran. "Though she often needs my help. I'm a detective, too, you know."

"Oh, I know," said Angela. "I don't doubt your abilities." Voices intruded upon their conversation and Angela pointed towards the door. "That's him now. Mr. Perfect. And if I'm not mistaken that's his less-than-perfect friend."

"The wastrel."

"The wastrel," Angela confirmed.

Gran moved towards the door and opened it a crack. She'd always been a great believer in snooping and eavesdropping as a way of catching criminals.

"You've changed," the wastrel was saying. "You've changed so much it's not funny anymore. And it's not just me that's saying it. They all do. Spiffy, Toddles, Pongo, Bertie. Even Bingo says you're not the man you used to be."

"Of course I've changed! I'm married, and a dad. What did you expect?"

"I expected you to be my best mate, mate. Not to chuck me the first chance you got. What does she have that I don't, eh?"

"Oh, for God's sakes. Don't make this about Tessa."

"I didn't make it about Tessa—you did, old chum. When you decided to get rid of fun Dante and turn into an old boring stiff."

"I'm still fun Dante, only now I'm having fun being a dad and a husband."

"Oh, booooring!"

"I think you better leave now, Damien."

"See? You're chucking me out!"

"I'm not chucking you out! I just don't want you to make a scene in front of my wife and daughter."

"I'm not making a scene. I'm just having a chat with my chum."

"Let's talk later, yeah?"

Tessa must have entered the room, for Damien cried, "There she is, the breaker-upper of friendships."

"Hello, Damien," said Tessa. "How are you?"

"Pitiful! Your husband doesn't even want to go to the pub with me."

"Well, I guess he's got other things to do."

"He's got you to do, you mean," said Damien darkly.

"Damien," said Dante warningly. "Don't talk to my wife like that."

"I'll talk to your wife any way I damn well please! This is all your fault, Tessa," said Damien, causing Angela, eavesdropping next to Gran, to raise a meaningful eyebrow.

"I never told Dante he couldn't see you."

"You don't have to! You've got him on such a tight leash he's turned into one of those pod people. A zombie. You've poisoned his mind against his best mates and now I don't even recognize him anymore!"

"And here I thought only women could make a scene," Gran whispered.

"Oh, men can do it better," said Angela. "And Damien is not the only one. Plenty of Dante's old friends are annoyed he doesn't hang out with them anymore. And they all blame Tessa, of course."

A security man must have been alerted by the noise, for Damien now said, "All right, all right! I'll go. You don't have to—ow! You're hurting me!"

"Please leave now, sir," said a deep voice.

"It's all right," said Dante. "Damien was just leaving, wasn't he?"

"No, I wasn't!"

"Call me, yeah?"

"Fat chance!" cried Damien. "And don't you dare call me, unless it is to apologize for your appalling behavior and that of your dreadful Goon McGoon." And just before he slammed the door, he added, "See you in hell!"

"Ouch," said Gran. "Looks like another candidate for our list of suspects."

"Oh, this one just hit the top of the list," said Angela. "And now for a more important question: who's going to shower first—you or me?"

$\mathcal{I}$'d escaped the living room when the brawl with the former friend of Dante's began to get loud. Dooley had joined me, while Harriet and Brutus had presumably taken a different route and were checking out some other part of the house in search of some peace and quiet.

Cats don't like loud. We like it when humans don't raise their voices or shout down the house. We don't like loud music either, or loud noises in general. Cars backfiring, fireworks or explosions: big no-no's in our world.

"This looks like a nice and quiet place," said Dooley.

"Yeah, I hope so," I said as we walked into what looked like an office of some kind. It was empty, which was a plus after the ruckus we'd endured.

"Who knew Dante had such obnoxious friends?" said Dooley.

"Not me."

We glanced around and to our elation found a nice and comfy-looking couch waiting for us in the office. Dooley and I shared a look of pleasant surprise and headed for the couch.

We soon made ourselves comfortable and were enjoying a nap when loud voices approached.

"Oh, no," said Dooley without opening his eyes.

"Maybe they won't come in," I said.

The voices grew louder, and then Tessa walked in, accompanied by a stern-looking woman with glasses, hair pulled back in a painful-looking bun.

"Maybe they won't stay," I said.

The two women settled themselves at a table next to the desk.

"Maybe they'll meditate," said Dooley.

But of course they launched into some kind of business meeting. The woman obviously was Tessa's assistant, for she had a whole list of stuff for Tessa to do. And as she read it out, Tessa was giving comments and adding her notes.

"Maybe we should find another place to nap," I said.

But then the assistant suddenly raised her voice.

"I'm not sure how much more of this I can take, Tessa. Please forgive me but I feel like I have to speak up now or I'll simply burst!"

"Please don't burst," Dooley muttered.

Tessa seemed taken aback. "But, Sherri," was the only thing she could think of to say.

"It's too much!" the woman practically squealed. "When you hired me away from the institute I was over the moon. But now I realize I was rash. I should have stayed put instead of rushing into this position without thinking."

"I think you're doing a great job. And I'm very happy with your work."

"Well, you certainly don't show it," said the woman prissily. "In fact you seem to relish every opportunity to criticize my work, tell me that what I'm doing doesn't give you satisfaction, and generally behave as if you know everything best and I'm just an annoying superfluous sidekick!"

"I'm so sorry you feel that way," said Tessa.

"Well, I do—and have for some time. Remember when I told you it would be a good idea if you and Dante launched your own Instagram? And you told me it was too soon? And then you went ahead and did it anyway. Without telling me? And you hired Sammy to handle the account?" She pressed a hand to her chest. "That was like a dagger to the heart, Tessa. A dagger to the heart!"

"I—I didn't mean to, Sherri. I just wanted to hire the best person to—"

"I'm the best!" said Sherri, wiping away tears. "And you treat me like dirt! That's how I feel anyway." She took a tissue from her sleeve and pressed it to her nose. "That said, I think we can both agree this has to end now."

"But, Sherri…" said Tessa feebly.

The assistant abruptly rose to her feet. "I bid you adieu." She stuck out her hand. "And I wish you well in all your future endeavors."

Tessa shook the woman's hand. She looked stunned.

Sherri gave a sad smile and touched Tessa's cheek. "I adored you—from afar—but now that I've come to know you, I can see you're a wonderful human being, and a terrible boss. Goodbye and good luck."

And with these words she turned on her heel and waltzed out, leaving her former employer to stare after her, shocked and visibly dismayed.

Tessa blinked and spotted us. "Maybe I should hire you as my personal assistants," she said finally. "I have a feeling you'd do a much better job and would be much easier to handle than all these so-called professionals."

And shaking her head, she walked out.

"Well, that was instructive," I said.

"Tessa doesn't seem to have much luck picking her staff," said Dooley.

"No, she does not."

"You think it's because she's tough to work for?"

"I don't know, Dooley. Maybe it's a cultural thing. Maybe the English have different expectations about what it's like to work for someone like Tessa who clearly seems to know what she wants and isn't afraid to express it."

"I hope her security people don't walk out, too, or else she won't have anyone to protect her."

"She will always have Fluffy," I said, which drew a smile from Dooley. "And us," I added, making Dooley's smile even wider.

"And of course there's always Dante," he said.

"Her knight in shining armor."

"Why shining armor, though, Max? Why does it have to shine?"

"I think it's just a phrase, Dooley. Any old armor will do. Though it's always nice to have a shining armor, of course. Nobody likes a scruffy and dented old armor."

"That's true," Dooley admitted.

Odelia came walking into the office and seemed relieved to see us. "Oh, there you are. I was wondering where you'd gone off to. Tessa is giving a speech in town. Do you guys want to come? Or do you want to stay here?"

Dooley and I shared a quick glance. "Stay here," we said in unison. At least with the humans out of the house, we might actually have a chance to sleep off this terrible jet lag!

CHAPTER 19

*I*t was a whole production but finally they managed to leave the cottage and be on their way. Dante and Tessa traveled in the first car, along with Tessa's cousin Nesbit and Angela, while Chase, Odelia and Gran traveled in the second car. There was a third car filled with security people, and all three cars had privacy glass so no one could look in and know in which car the royal couple traveled.

"If we're unlucky they'll think we're Dante and Tessa and start shooting at us," said Gran, who looked nervous.

"I'm sure they won't," said Odelia, though she didn't feel entirely relaxed herself.

"Did you catch that big altercation with the best friend?" asked Chase.

"I did," said Odelia.

"I did, too," said Gran. "What a jerk, right?"

"Well, I can imagine it must be tough on Dante's former friends to see him change so much."

"Yeah, but that's only to be expected. I mean, the guy wasn't always going to be the fun-loving rogue all his life."

"He could have been," said Chase. "Some guys are like that. They never change."

"I think it speaks for Dante that he changed. He grew up and got a life! What's so bad about that?"

"It's bad because his friends are now confronted with the ugly truth about themselves," said Chase. "They're confronted with the fact that while they're still acting like a bunch of irresponsible teenagers, Dante is now a grownup."

"That's probably what hurts the most," said Odelia. "Not the fact that they lost a friend, but he's holding up a mirror. And they don't like what they see."

"They didn't have to lose Dante as a friend," said Gran. "They could have stayed friends, if only they'd grown up alongside him. Become men."

"Truer words have never been spoken," said Odelia, and eyed her grandmother approvingly. "Look at you. Being all smart and wise."

"I'm always wise and smart," said Gran.

"I know, but you're acting more mature, all of a sudden. No more weird hobbies or crazy stunts."

Gran smiled. "There comes a time in everyone's life when you have to decide whether to go through life like a human wrecking ball or be a force for good. And I've chosen to be a force for good, spreading sweetness and light."

"Oh, that's deep," said Chase.

"That's because I'm a deep person."

Odelia wasn't sure if it was temporary or permanent, but she liked this new and improved Gran. "I like it," she said. "I mean, I'll always love you whatever you do, but I think this is definitely a better and kinder you."

Gran sighed and gave her granddaughter a wan smile. "Life gives you kicks in the groin sometimes, and it's at moments like these that you have to decide whether to turn those kicks into lemons or not."

"I think the expression is that when life gives you lemons, you make lemonade," said Chase.

"Oh, Chase. You say it so well," said Gran, placing her hands in her lap and nodding beatifically. She then raised her hand, and waved at the passing scenery. "I'm going to let you in on a little secret."

"Oh? What's that?" asked Chase.

"I'm going to be Queen."

Chase and Odelia both blinked. "What?"

"That's right. It's one of the reasons I was so keen to come along on this trip. America deserves a queen and I'm going to be it. Her. She. Whatever."

"But we don't have a queen," said Odelia.

"Exactly! And now we will." She smiled. "Moi."

"You don't understand. We don't have a queen because we are a republic. We have a president, not a monarch like a lot of these European countries."

"And don't you think it's time we put a stop to that? America needs a queen. Not these bozos that come and go and make a mess of things. A nice queen would give the country some much-needed stability, not to mention international prestige. And you can be heir to my throne," she said graciously, extending a hand to Odelia.

"If you're the queen, Marge will be crown princess," said Chase. "That's how it usually works."

"I'm going to skip a generation and make Odelia queen."

"Marge won't like it," said Chase.

Gran waved an imperious hand. "Marge will be fine. It's Tex that I'm worried about. Can you imagine having Tex as king? That simply won't do. No, when I'm done being queen, in thirty years or so, I'll abdicate the throne and make you queen, Odelia. Of course you'll have to change your name. Queen Odelia just doesn't have that ring to it. You'd have to choose something regal. Like Eleanor. Or Mathilde."

"Tell me you're joking, Gran," said Odelia.

"I'm dead serious! America's getting its queen and I'm going to ask the British queen for a couple of pointers and useful tips of the trade."

"It's not gonna happen," said Chase. "You'd have to rewrite the constitution. Heck, you'd have to change the whole system."

"Systems can be changed, and constitutions can be rewritten. I'll ask my future colleague the Queen to put in a good word for me."

"A good word won't make it happen, Gran," said Odelia. "You can't be queen. And if you try, everybody's gonna think you're a crackpot."

"Nonsense. The moment we get back, I'm going to Washington and tell them to call off the next election. I'm sure they'll all be very happy. Elections are tough, not to mention expensive. A queen is a much cheaper option."

Odelia couldn't argue with that part.

"What are you going to tell them in Washington?" asked Chase, who seemed to think the whole thing was a big joke.

"I'll just tell them: Your queen is here. You may bow now."

"They'll probably kick you out," said Chase with a laugh.

"No, they won't. I'll convince them to give it a shot."

Odelia remembered they'd all watched *Mr. Smith Goes to Washington* the other day. That was probably where Gran had gotten the idea.

"Gran, you don't know the first thing about being a queen!" she said.

"Or politics," Chase added.

"Which is why I'm going to ask the Queen to give me some tips," said Gran patiently. "The woman has been queen for so long she knows a thing or two about the job and will only be too happy to help out an aspiring royal."

"Oh, dear God," said Odelia, leaning her head back

against the leather headrest. "And here I thought you'd finally gone sane."

"I have gone sane. Even better. I've gone queen."

"Gran, you simply can't—"

But Gran wagged her finger. "What's with all this 'Gran' business? You'll address me as Your Royal Highness from now on."

"But Gran!"

But Gran tilted her chin and looked away.

"All right—Your Royal Highness!"

Gran looked up, comporting herself very regally indeed. "Yes?"

"What will Mom and Dad say?"

Gran lifted her shoulders in a queenly shrug. "Let them eat cake."

CHAPTER 20

*T*he meeting took place at a shelter for homeless people, and Tessa was clearly in her element. Accompanied by Dante, and watched over by an ever-vigilant Angela, she talked to several of the homeless present, the people who ran the center, and a selected group of reporters snapping shots and filming the whole thing for the evening news. Wherever Tessa went, film crews followed. She was a lightning rod for their attention, her presence electrifying. Dressed soberly in a simple black dress, she played her role to perfection, showing genuine affection for the shabbily clothed vagrants.

Dante, who stood next to Odelia, gleamed with pride.

"She's amazing, isn't she?" said Odelia.

"She is. She's grown in the role and handles it all with such grace."

"I think she's wonderful, no matter what the media people say."

The gleam diminished as Dante locked eyes with Otis Robbins for a moment, then looked away. "It's tragic the media would choose to turn my wife into a target. Especially as she's the most wonderful person I've ever met and the terrible things they write about her are lies, every single one of them."

"I must say that not all the media are against her, though," said Chase, gesturing to several members of the press who smiled and applauded as Tessa placed a kiss on an elderly woman's cheeks, much to the woman's glee.

"No, of course not. But it's people like Otis Robins who don't seem to grasp that we have a real opportunity here. An opportunity to change the way we royals interact with the public. On an equal footing, I mean."

Odelia watched as Tessa's smile was infectious, and reflected in the smiles of the people she met. "I think it's true what they say about her," she said.

"What's that?"

"Despised by the media barons, loved by the people."

"That's exactly true. Which just goes to show that whatever they write about her, the vast majority of the population sees right through those lies."

"Her rise has certainly been meteoric," said Chase. "Until a few months ago I'd never even heard of Tessa Torrance."

Dante looked up sharply. "What do you mean? She's Odelia's cousin."

Oops! "What Chase means is that I never told him about her," said Odelia.

"Right. And why is that?" asked Dante, a little crossly, it seemed.

"It's complicated," said Odelia. "Family stuff. You know."

Dante nodded. "Oh, I do know. Family is both the most wonderful and most frustrating thing in the world."

"It is," said Odelia, staring at her grandmother, who stood practicing her regal poise, and had started waving to anyone who would pay her attention.

Tessa now called for silence. "I would like to say a few

words," she said with an engaging smile. "I think what you're doing here at the center is both important and incredibly inspiring. And being with you here today has certainly inspired me to do more—to be more. I can't imagine the situations some of you have endured, and the courage it must have taken you to live through them and still be the amazing, gracious people you clearly are."

And she would probably have said more, if not suddenly there was a loud crack, and suddenly something seemed to explode behind Tessa. And then all hell broke loose, as more cracks sounded, which Odelia now recognized as shots being fired. Tessa and all those present ducked for cover while the people from her security team all huddled around her, keeping her safe.

People were screaming and yelling and as Chase growled, "Too bad I couldn't bring my gun!" suddenly the lights in the room were doused and for a moment it seemed as if fear was the only thing Odelia knew.

Being on the floor, in the dark, a crazed shooter on the loose, she flashed back to the most crucial times in her life. And as she lay there, Chase right next to her, she suddenly heard herself ask, "Chase, if we make it out of here alive— will you marry me?"

"We will make it out of here alive," he said, "and yes, I will marry you. But damn it, you kinda stole my thunder, Poole!"

"I'm sorry! I just thought if I don't ask now maybe we'll both be dead and I'll regret not asking!"

"When you're dead you have no regrets. Or at least that's the consensus."

"I know! I'm not thinking straight right now."

"Thinking straight or not, I'm going to walk you down that aisle, babe, and I'm going to kiss the bride, if it's the last thing I do!"

"Me, too!"

Suddenly the lights in the room flashed on again, and when Odelia glanced around, her eyes adjusting to the light, she saw that Tessa was still alive, and seemingly not hurt. Dante was with her, and he, too, seemed to be all right.

Gran, meanwhile, said, "Will someone save your queen, for God's sakes!"

She was stuck to the floor, a rather voluminous lady pinning her down.

Chase removed the lady by yanking her up, thereby saving 'his queen.'

"Thank you, my loyal subject," she said, and extended a hand for him to kiss.

"Oh, for crying out loud," he grunted.

"Hey—I could hold you in contempt!" she shouted.

Police came charging into the room, and one by one everyone was led out.

"Did you get the shooter?" asked Odelia when she found herself being jostled out along with Tessa's cousin Nesbit, the beefy security man.

"No, we didn't," he said, looking grim. "But by God, we will. And when we do, he's going to wish he was never born."

CHAPTER 21

*W*hen Tessa and Dante piled into the house, followed by Angela, Chase, Odelia and Gran, they were all atwitter. Apparently something had happened.

"What's wrong?" I asked, lifting my head from my paws. I'd put in a solid couple of hours of sleep and I was slowly starting to feel like myself again.

"There's been another attack," said Odelia as she sat down next to us on the couch. Tessa switched on the TV, and we could all see firsthand the pandemonium at the homeless shelter. People were screaming, shots were being fired, and suddenly the lights went out and the place went dark. A grave-looking newscaster announced that the Duke and Duchess of Essex were safe, but that for a while there things had looked very hairy indeed.

"It's a miracle you made it out alive," I said, riveted by the images.

"Turns out it was just firecrackers set off by a couple of kids. At least that's what the police are saying. There actually was an attack, only Tessa opted not to tell the police, for the same reasons she mentioned earlier."

Tessa and Dante were conferring with Angela, and judging from the heated argument they weren't seeing eye to eye.

"So there was an attack?" I asked, greatly concerned.

"While the lights were out, Tessa says she felt something graze her cheek."

Odelia was right. There was a band-aid on Tessa's cheek.

"Someone fired a shot at her but missed," said Odelia.

"Could whoever is responsible set off the fireworks?"

"Possibly. They say it was kids, but I'm not convinced. More likely the killer paid them off to create confusion, then cut the power to cover his tracks."

"Did they find out who was responsible?"

She shook her head. "There were a lot of people there. The moment those firecrackers hit the place descended into chaos."

Gran cranked up the volume on the TV. "Listen to this," she said, and everyone's attention turned to the screen.

"There are rumors this may have been an attempt on the Duchess of Essex's life," said the newscaster in the same mournful tone, "but a statement has just been issued claiming those rumors to be absolutely false."

"Oh, for goodness sakes," Dante said under his breath.

"Through an unfortunate concatenation of circumstances the Duchess suffered a minor injury but at no time was she in any danger, real or imagined," the newscaster continued reading the royal statement.

"Who issued this bogus statement?" asked Dante. "That's what I would like to know."

"I did," said Tessa.

"Someone tried to shoot you! I was there! I heard the shot!"

"No damage was done," she said, touching the band-aid on her cheek.

"This is serious, Tessa," he said, concern lacing his voice. "Someone took a shot at you. And now I'm starting to wonder if that stone ball that fell on you was an accident or a deliberate attempt on your life."

"There was a third attempt," said Angela suddenly.

"Mom!" Tessa said, aghast. "I thought we agreed—"

"I think it's time you told your husband, honey."

"But you said—"

"I know what I said. But I've changed my mind. Dante was standing right next to me when that shot was fired, and he was as shocked as I was."

"He was standing next to me when that ball almost fell on me. You said he was probably working with an accomplice."

Dante looked shocked. "What?!"

Angela took a deep breath. "Dante, someone tried to poison your wife's tea. Also, Odelia isn't actually Tessa's cousin and Vesta isn't her grandmother."

Dante looked flabbergasted, his face taking on a scarlet hue. "She's not your cousin? So who is she? And why has she been staying under our roof?"

"I can explain," said Tessa with an exasperated look at her mother, who pulled an 'I'm sorry, honey' face.

It took Tessa a while to tell the story but she told it well, and by the end of the convoluted tale, Dante looked even more worried than before.

"We have to tell the police," was his first reaction. "ASAP."

"That's exactly what I don't want," said Tessa. "No one can know."

"But—"

"What's going to happen if people become aware there's somebody trying to kill me?"

"They'll be stopped!"

"No, it's going to turn into a huge scandal—one that will be plastered across all the front pages and dominate several news cycles. Your family will be faced with an enormously embarrassing episode."

"So? At least you'll be safe."

"It's attention we don't need—attention we don't want."

"We don't control the media, Tessa. They'll write what they write."

"I know, but I want people to pay attention to us for the right reasons. For the work that we do. The charities we support. The message we want to convey. I don't want us to become the couple hounded by a would-be assassin. It's going to define us and it's going to define your family and mine and we don't need that kind of publicity."

"So you're telling me to just sit back and do nothing?!"

"No, of course not. That's where Odelia comes in. She's handled this type of situation before, and is on the verge of catching whoever's behind this." She directed a questioning look at Odelia, who nodded.

"We're making progress," she confirmed curtly.

"Have you at least some idea who this person is?" Dante asked.

"We're closing in on a suspect," Odelia said after a moment's hesitation.

Dante narrowed his eyes at her. "You don't have a clue, do you?"

"Not an inkling," Odelia confessed.

Dante dragged a hand through his thinning ginger mane. "Oh, God. This is a nightmare. And why didn't you tell me this before?!"

"That's on me," said Angela. "You were one of my main suspects."

"You actually thought I would kill my wife? Are you crazy?"

Angela shrugged. "I just figured that with all the negative

publicity Tessa has been getting, you might want to get rid of her."

"By murdering her?!"

"I figured that's the way you royals dealt with trouble-some spouses."

"We're Windsors, Angela. Not the Corleones."

Angela rolled her eyes. "Oh, pipe down, Dante. It's not as if you haven't given me reason to suspect you. You keep getting into fights with Tessa. And you keep telling her she needs to adapt. I just figured you were already looking for a way out of this marriage, and seeing how you royals are allergic to even a whiff of scandal a nice 'accident' just might do the trick for you."

"I don't believe this," he said, shaking his head with exas-peration.

Just then, one of the guards approached the royal couple. "You have visitors, sir."

"Tell them we're a little busy right now," said Dante.

"It's your brother and his wife, the Duke and Duchess of Bristol."

CHAPTER 22

"This is so exciting!" Harriet said.

"Why?" asked Brutus, at a loss.

"Are you crazy? It's the future king and queen paying us a visit!"

"Oh, okay," said Brutus, not convinced.

The future king and queen walked into the house, their faces masks of concern. Jeremy was a tall, thin man with thinning mane, while his wife Jennie was a kind-faced, rangy brunette. When she saw Tessa, Jennie immediately streaked forward, arms outstretched. "Oh, you poor thing. Are you all right?"

"I'm fine," said Tessa with a strained smile. The events of the past couple of days had clearly left a big impression on her, and her customary sunny disposition had suffered.

"This is so awful! Do they know what happened?"

"Kids setting off firecrackers and a fuse box meltdown," she said automatically, as if reading from a teleprompter. "The whole thing gave us a big scare. But nothing bad happened. Just a concatenation of circumstances."

"Yes, I heard just now—you must have been terrified."

"It was pretty scary," Tessa admitted.

Meanwhile Jeremy clapped his brother on the shoulder. "Gave you quite a fright, the whole dreadful business, what?"

"It did," Dante admitted. He clamped his lips together, clearly wanting to say more and being in two minds about Tess's information embargo.

"Kids, eh?" said Jeremy. "Blimey."

"What are you going to do?"

"Lock them up in the Tower?" Jeremy suggested, eliciting a weak smile from his younger brother.

Jeremy directed a worried look at him. "Are you sure you're all right?"

"Yes, of course."

"You don't look all right. I'd say you look... awfully pissed off."

"Well, I am," said Dante. "How would you feel if your wife was suddenly under attack."

"From firecrackers?"

"We didn't know it was firecrackers. It sounded like gunfire."

Jeremy smiled indulgently. "Surely an ex-military man like yourself can tell the difference between a firecracker and gunfire?"

"I didn't know what to think. Everybody hit the floor and there was panic for a few moments, especially when the lights went out immediately after."

"Shock to the system, eh?" said Jeremy knowingly. "Good for you, old chap. Brings out the old fighting spirit. Makes you feel alive. Speaking of which, I've heard through the grapevine Gran is on her way over."

"Oh, dear God, no," Dante groaned.

Gran, who'd heard her name mentioned, pricked up her hears. "Excuse me," she said, approaching the two brothers. "Who's on her way here?"

111

"Our grandmother," said Dante. "Oh, I'm so sorry. Where are my manners? Vesta Muffin, this is my brother, the Duke of Bristol."

"Please call me Jeremy," said Jeremy graciously.

But Gran wasn't interested in niceties or social decorum. "Are you telling me the Queen of England is on her way over here?"

"Yup," said Jeremy. "She must have heard about the incident at the shelter and wants to see for herself what the fuss is all about. I honestly believe this goes to show your security people don't know their arse from their elbow. What an astonishing cock-up."

"They couldn't have foreseen something like this would happen," said Dante, though I could tell he was thinking the same thing his brother was thinking.

"They could have performed a sweep of the room. Confiscated those blasted firecrackers. Made certain those little blighters weren't anywhere near you or Tessa. And then there's the fuse box. They should have checked."

"You're probably right," said Dante.

"Of course I'm right! Who's in charge of your security?"

"Kingsley Para."

"I'd take a long hard look at his credentials. And talk to Protection Command. There should be consequences to a disaster like this."

"I will," said Dante. "Trouble is, one of the security people is actually Tessa's cousin. And she tells me he's quite good at what he does."

"Well, obviously he's not, is he, old boy? I'd think about chucking him—family or no family. Can't have nepotism stand in the way of keeping safe."

"What's nepotism, Max?" asked Dooley.

"When you give an unfair advantage to members of your family in the distribution of jobs and such," I said. "Like when the president of a country appoints friends and family to important jobs, without following procedure."

"Like if Tessa would make Fluffy her head of security?"

"Maybe she should," said Brutus. "Prince Jeremy is right. What a screwup."

"Could it be that her security team is in on this?" I asked.

"You mean, could they be working with the killer?" asked Harriet.

"It would explain how he got through security just now, and managed to fire off a shot. And how he got into the house and laced her tea with Belladonna. Or sneak past security to tip over that stone ball."

"It would explain a lot," Brutus agreed.

"But wouldn't her cousin know if a conspiracy was being hatched?" asked Harriet.

"Not if he's in on it," I said.

We all glanced up at Tessa, who was keeping it together, even though the strain the incident had caused showed on her face and her rigid posture.

"I think Odelia should have a chat with the cousin," I said.

We agreed to bring it up as soon as Odelia was done talking to the Duchess of Bristol, aka Jennie, but then a loud noise told us another visitor had arrived.

And judging from Gran's excited cries, it was none other than the Queen!

CHAPTER 23

$\mathcal{I}$t was a great honor and a wonderful opportunity to meet the one and only Queen, of course, but what I was looking most forward to was meeting those famous corgis, and I sincerely hoped she'd brought them along.

"So you better be on your best behavior," said Harriet, suddenly deciding she was the one in charge. "No backtalk and no foul language from any of you—is that understood?"

"I don't think the Queen speaks our language," Dooley pointed out.

"Obviously I'm not talking about the Queen," said Harriet. "I'm talking about her precious corgis. Be polite and show them the respect they deserve."

"Oh, for crying out loud," said Brutus. "They're just dogs!"

"They're royal dogs. And they just happen to be the most famous dogs in the world. People even make movies about them, so they're not 'just dogs.' They're brothers and sisters and we need to be on our best behavior. Show them we're not the country bumpkins they probably take us for. That we're worthy of being in their royal presence. Basking in their glow. Moving in their sophisticated circles."

Brutus clearly wasn't in agreement, but there was no time to complain, for the door swung open and there she was: the Queen, resplendent in fluorescent pink. Pink dress, pink coat and pink hat. She clutched her famous purse, the one she uses to signal her staff when she needs to be rescued from garrulous and annoying company, her face split in a wide, full-toothed smile.

"She has such nice teeth," Dooley marveled. "Will you look at those snappers? They're absolutely perfect."

"Not her own, probably," I said. "Humans tend to lose their teeth, and then have them replaced with new ones made of plastic."

"Plastic teeth? How weird," said Dooley.

"It's true, though. Grandma has fake teeth."

"Oh, that's right," said Dooley. "I've seen her take them out."

We watched in fascination as Gran actually curtsied before the Queen, and showed her own, almost identical, choppers to the beloved monarch.

"Such an honor," Gran gushed. "I've been meaning to ask you, Your Highness, if you could spare a few moments of your precious time, could you perhaps give me a couple of pointers on how to be a queen?"

The Queen gave her a curious look. "Whatever do you mean, Mrs. Vesta?"

"Well, the thing is—I'm going to be queen myself, you see. Over in America. And since you've held the job for so long now, I'm sure you're perfectly positioned to help a newbie get started on her queenly tenure."

The Queen's left eyebrow quivered slightly, expressing surprise. "You're going to be Queen of America?"

"Yes, I am. I've got it all worked out. See, the presidential system we got now isn't cutting it anymore. Too fickle for a great nation like ours. What we need is a queen, who will rise above the political fray and all those bickering politicians. And there's no one better suited for the role than me. Besides which, it was my idea, so I got first dibs. And then of course I'm giving the throne to Odelia—I'm skipping a generation, you see, mainly because my son-in-law is a jackass and he'd only ruin things if he became king."

"Very wise," said the Queen, then leaned in and said, under her breath, "I've been thinking along those same lines myself, quite frankly."

"Great minds think alike!" said Gran, eliciting a chuckle from the monarch.

The Queen approached Tessa with outstretched arms. "Oh, my dear, dear Tessa. What an ordeal you have suffered through. Are you all right?"

"I'm fine, Ma'am," said Tessa.

The Queen tsk-tsked. "How many times have I told you not to call me that? It's Gam-Gam!"

"Yes... Gam-Gam," said Tessa, struggling to get the words across her larynx.

"So you were attacked, is that it?" The Queen asked, giving Tessa a keen look.

"Oh, no, nothing like that," Tessa assured the older woman. "Just kids playing a prank."

"Oh, dear. Kids these days. They will go too far." She lightly touched Tessa's cheek. "You're hurt, I see."

"Nothing serious," Tessa was quick to say. "Just a graze."

"From the firecrackers?"

"No, I must have hit something when I dropped to the floor."

"Very distressing," the Queen said. "Very distressing

indeed." She then cut a curious glance to Odelia and Chase. "I do hope you're making progress on your inquiries," she said vaguely.

"Inquiries?" inquired Odelia.

"A little birdie told me you're here on Angela's instigation to look into certain… allegations." She sighed. "I do hope you will move your investigation along quite speedily. At my age one wants nothing more than to see one's family happy and safe from harm."

"One knows," said Harriet, sounding surprised. "One actually knows!"

"One what?" asked Dooley.

"The Queen! She knows!"

"Knows what?" asked Brutus.

"She knows that Odelia is here to investigate the assassination attempts!"

"Impossible," I said. "Angela told no one."

"She must have a spy somewhere," said Harriet. "I heard the Queen has her spies everywhere."

"I'm sure she's just talking in general terms about Tessa's safety. Tessa is, after all, the mother of the Queen's great-grandchild."

"No, I'm sure she knows," Harriet insisted. "Oh, one is good."

"Two is better, though, right?" said Dooley.

"Oh, Dooley," sighed Harriet. "Please go away."

"Where are the corgis?" asked Dooley now.

I'd been asking myself the same question. The corgis seemed to be nowhere to be found.

"Let's look outside," Harriet suggested. "This is our one and only chance to meet the famous corgis and I'm not going to miss it!"

We all hopped from the couch and made our way out the

door. A black Range Rover was parked right outside, the door open. Inside, three corgis sat waiting patiently for their human's return.

So Harriet, being Harriet, wasted no time and introduced herself.

"Hello there, Your Royal Highnesses," she said, doing a little curtsy. "My name is Harriet, and I'm so very, very pleased to finally meet you!"

The corgis, who looked very similar, were unimpressed.

"You're a cat," said the first corgi.

"Excellent powers of observation," said Harriet without a trace of irony. "I am, indeed, a cat, and I'm also your biggest fan."

"Cats usually aren't the biggest fans of dogs," the corgi pointed out. She was speaking a little huffily, I thought, but Harriet wasn't deterred.

"Oh, but you're not just any dogs. You're the Queen's corgis!"

The corgi darted a look at me and Brutus and Dooley.

"Hi," I said when I felt the corgi's curious glance rake my visage. "My name is Max, and I'm Odelia's cat. Odelia is a friend of the Duchess and Duke of Essex and we're all guests at their cottage."

"You're friends of Tessa's?" asked the corgi, quirking an imperious eyebrow.

"That's right. And we're also friends of Fluffy. Tessa and Dante's dog?"

The corgi gave me a supercilious smile. "Of course you would be friends with that runt."

I had the distinct impression these weren't the nicest, sweetest dogs. Fame must have gone to their heads. The same thought occurred to Brutus, for he muttered, "What a stuck-up little—"

"I beg your pardon?" The corgi said, raising her voice. She might be stuck-up but she had excellent hearing.

"I was just saying how Odelia is working on a *mockup* of Newtmore Cottage," said Brutus. "Odelia wants to build a cottage just like this one."

"Is this Odelia person an architect?"

"No, she's—"

"A contractor?"

"No, she's actually—"

"An interior designer? A builder?"

"Um…"

"Then why would she spend her time creating mockups?"

"Oh, do be nice to the cats," said the second corgi.

I now saw that the corgis had their names in gold-plated tags dangling from their collars. The nasty corgi answered to the name Sweetie, the second one was called Fräulein and the third one Molly.

"Tessa's friends are our friends," said Fräulein now.

Molly chimed in, "Any friend of the Duchess of Essex is a friend of ours. Hop in, cats, and tell us what the word on the street is."

In spite of the fact that I disliked the corgis, I didn't want to miss a chance of sitting in the royal vehicle—in the exact same spot the Queen sat! So I hopped in, and so did Harriet, Brutus and Dooley. I have to admit the leather seats were amazing. Soft to the tush and yet firm. Also, the car smelled to lavender.

"They're not street cats, Molly," said Sweetie. "Didn't you pay attention? Their human is a mockup artist." Her voice dripped with disdain.

"I thought *all* cats were street cats," said Molly.

"Not all cats, surely. Some cats are domesticated. Though they tend to be adopted by commoners, of course. No royal wants to be seen dead with a cat."

"Just the idea. Imagine a royal with a cat. How perfectly horrid!"

Both cats laughed, until Fräulein said, "Please be nice to the cats. I'm sure they have stories to tell, so let's hear them out. How are you finding your stay at Newtmore Cottage, cat?" she asked, enunciating every word as if talking to a toddler.

"So far our stay has been perfectly satisfactory," I said, adopting the same tone.

The corgi smiled at her cohorts. "See? These are clearly intelligent creatures with a certain capacity for conversation."

"Hey, look here," said Brutus, starting to get a little hot under his collar, "I'm not going to be insulted by a bunch of stuck-up, nasty—"

"I knew you said stuck-up and not mockup!" said Sweetie.

"We're not stupid," said Brutus. "We can tell when we're being insulted. And you've been insulting us from the moment you laid eyes on us."

"Please, feel free to leave anytime," said Sweetie, tilting her chin. "In fact, now that I come to think of it..." She sniffed the air. "My sensitive nose has suddenly detected a rather unpleasant smell pervading this fine automobile."

"Are you suggesting we stink?" Brutus growled.

"I'm suggesting you get out of the car, cat." Then she leaned in, giving Brutus a dirty look. "Or, to say it in your street lingo, get lost!"

And we would have gotten lost, if not the door had suddenly been slammed shut, the car put in gear and we were surprised to find we were on the move.

"What's going on?" I asked.

But the corgis looked too stunned to respond.

Fräulein was staring at the driver, then stammered, "That's not Bart!"

As if he understood, the man turned and smiled a yellow-toothed grin at us. "Brace yourselves, pooches—this is a kidnapping!" And to prove he wasn't kidding, he stomped down on the accelerator and the car lurched forward.

We were being abducted—along with the Queen's corgis!

CHAPTER 24

"*U*m, what's happening?" asked Sweetie.

"I think you guys are being kidnapped," said Harriet.

"Not just them," I said. "We're being kidnapped right alongside them!"

Oh, boy. This wasn't good. I'd never been kidnapped before, but I had a sinking feeling I wasn't going to like it.

"Kidnapped?" said Sweetie as if the concept was alien to her. "What do you mean, kidnapped?"

"It's when they take you against your will and then they ask money to let you go," Dooley explained patiently. He glanced to me. "It was on the Discovery Channel. There was this rich girl who was kidnapped, and then she started to really like her kidnapper. I think she even wanted to marry him."

I studied the driver, who was chewing gum with his mouth open and tapping the wheel with a dirty fingernail. No way was I marrying this guy.

"But... we can't be kidnapped!" said Sweetie. "That just

doesn't happen to us. We're the Queen's corgis! The Queen's corgis simply don't get kidnapped!"

"Well, you are now," said Brutus, who seemed to derive a certain satisfaction from the fact.

"This is all your fault, cat," Sweetie told him viciously. "We meet you and five minutes later we are being kidnapped. Coincidence? I think not!"

"We had nothing to do with this!" said Brutus.

"Yes, we're victims just as much as you guys," said Harriet.

"So how are we going to handle this?" I asked. I frowned at the door. "Does this thing open? Where's the handle?"

"It's fully automated," said Fräulein. "There is no handle."

Our jabbering must have alerted the driver, for he looked over his shoulder. "Hey, you're cats," he said.

"Well spotted, sir," I said. "Well spotted."

The guy wasn't happy about this development, though, for he grabbed his phone and began tapping it furiously.

"Hey—no texting and driving!" Sweetie called out.

"I think we have bigger issues than road safety right now," said Fräulein. "If these cats are right, we've just been dognapped. Which means they'll want to ask money for us and they'll lock us up until the Queen agrees to pay up."

"Oh, but of course she'll agree," said Sweetie. "We're her precious corgis! She'd never let anything bad happen to us. Would she?"

"Of course not," said Molly.

"I'm not so sure," said Fräulein. "Last time I checked the Queen is winding down her corgi-producing extravaganza. I'll bet she is switching breeds."

"Switching breeds!" cried Sweetie. "She wouldn't!"

"She would. In a changing world it's important for a public figure like the Queen to stay relevant. Keeping things fresh. Maybe she'd like to adopt a Chihuahua for a change?

Or a Maltipoo? Or even a micro teacup Poodle. Those teacup dogs are all the rage right now. I hear Katy Perry has one."

"Who cares what Katy Perry has!" said her colleague. "The Queen would never trade us in for a bunch of... dumb animals!"

"We're animals, too," Molly reminded her.

"We're not animals! We're corgis!"

"Listen, I got a problem," the driver spoke into his phone. "No, yeah, I got the dogs, but there's four cats in with them, innit? Yeah, *cats*. So what am I supposed to do with four cats? That wasn't part of the deal. Throw them out?"

"I don't like where this is going," said Dooley, and I agreed. Being thrown out of a moving vehicle sounded like a perfectly painful proposition.

The driver glanced back at us. "You mean, just dump em. Great. Yeah, whatever, bruv." He disconnected and drove on in silence for a while, then looked back at us, and said, probably more to himself than to us, "They're telling me to dump you guys. But I don't think I'm going to do that. I like animals, you see. I mean, it doesn't look like I do but I do. Which is why I'm going to take you along and maybe keep you for myself. Or I could sell you. Nice-looking cats such as yourselves, I'm pretty sure you'll fetch a pretty penny." He turned to look at the road again, much to my relief. "Yeah, that's what I'll do. I'll sell them. And maybe keep just one. I'll keep the fat red one. Fat red cats bring luck. Everybody knows that."

I glanced at the others, suddenly panicky. "Is he talking about me?"

"Do you see any other red fat cats?" Brutus asked with a nasty undertone.

I looked around. A white Persian, a butch black cat, a gray cat and three corgis. "No, I don't," I said weakly.

"So?" said Brutus.

"But I'm not fat! I'm big-boned. And I'm not red, I'm blorange!"

"Tell that to the guy," Brutus suggested. "I'm sure he'll want to know."

"What's blorange?" asked Fräulein curiously.

"It doesn't exist," said Brutus, still on his nasty streak.

"It does! It's pastel red with orange shades of peach and rose gold. Very popular with the influencers."

"I'll bet it is," said Sweetie, and it didn't sound like a compliment.

"Who cares?!" Harriet cried. "Let's focus, shall we? We're being kidnapped, and they're going to trade you in for a lot of money, and they're going to get rid of the rest of us."

"Except for Max," said Brutus. "They're going to keep him for luck." Somehow his words seemed to suggest I was in cahoots with the kidnapper!

"I don't want to be kept for luck!" I said.

"No, but you will—while he's going to sell the rest of us on Craigslist."

"Do they have Craigslist in England?" asked Harriet.

"Whatever! Our cushy lives are over, you guys! We'll probably end up living with some toothless degenerate inbred pervert in the Cotswolds!"

"Breathe," I said. "We have to breathe and think this through." I tried to slow my breathing. In and out. In and out. It wasn't working!

"And to think I dreamed all my life about meeting the Queen's corgis," lamented Harriet.

"You have?" asked Sweetie, sounding surprised.

Harriet nodded sadly. "And look where it got me. In the hands of a maniac!"

CHAPTER 25

"Oh, goodness me," said the Queen, clutching a hand to her heart. "Oh, dear goodness me. My corgis! My precious corgis!"

She was on the verge of collapsing to the floor, and the people who formed her entourage quickly stepped to the fore and deposited her on the couch, where she was taking little gulps of breath and was trying to steady herself.

"My cats," said Odelia, as she thought with a pang of sorrow of her sweet foursome. "They kidnapped my cats."

The entourage, clearly afraid she might keel over, too, took her by the arm and deposited her right next to the Queen. Gran, viewing this with a touch of rancor, now said, "My cats! Oh, dear goodness me, my cats!" and clasped an arm to her brow, then dropped herself down on Odelia's lap.

Odelia scooted over to make space, and now Gran was seated right next to the Queen.

"This is terrible," said the Queen. "Horrible! My precious sweet babies. They won't know what's going on. They will be apoplectic with anxiety!"

"They'll be fine," said what appeared to be the Queen's

senior aide, a man with gray hair so sculpted it looked as if he'd actually created it out of bitumen and glued it to his head. He was wearing some of those fashionable glasses that would have met the approval of Sir Elton John.

"But how is this possible?" asked the Queen. "How did this happen?"

"Bart stepped out for a smoke," said the aide, then coughed into his fist. "Before he knew what happened, a man dressed like him jumped into the car and drove off with it. Unfortunately Bart had left the engine running."

"But surely you are in pursuit. Please tell me you're in hot pursuit."

It was funny to hear the Queen use words like 'hot pursuit,' Odelia thought, even if the situation wasn't a funny one at all.

"I'm afraid we lost a vital opportunity there, Ma'am," said the aide, once again coughing into his fist. It seemed to be a favorite mannerism of his.

"Have you notified the police? Are *they* in pursuit? Have they taken out the helicopter? The drones? Tell me they're doing *something*!"

"I've notified Scotland Yard. They're sending a unit as soon as possible."

"Oh, dear goodness me," said the Queen, sagging into the couch "This is the worst thing that has ever happened to me. Positively the worst."

"If this is a kidnapping, they'll call in their demands any moment now," said Dante, looking grave. First the attempt on Tessa's life and now this.

Odelia wondered if the two events were connected somehow. She couldn't see how, though.

"Maybe we need to take matters into our own hands," said Chase.

"What do you suggest, young man?" said the Queen.

"I suggest we go in pursuit right now. They can't have gotten far."

"Oh, yes! Please do something!" said the Queen, quite unqueenly.

Chase and Odelia volunteered to be on the 'Hot Pursuit' team, and hurried out of the cottage. The Queen's driver Bart got behind the wheel of a second Range Rover, and soon they were moving along at a fast clip, zooming through the leafy lanes of the Newtmore Estate.

Bart, a stringy man with wispy yellow hair, consulted his GPS. "There's a fork in the road just up ahead," he said. "Where do you suggest we go?"

Odelia thought for a moment. She had an almost mystical connection with her cats, that much was true, but all it really amounted to was that she had the gift of the feline gab, nothing more. Could she somehow intuit which way Max and the others were being taken? She doubted it, but she had to try. For her cats' sake as well as the corgis.

"Left," she finally said, deciding to trust her gut.

The car swerved to the left, and the leafy lane merged onto a two-lane road. She was surprised when Bart steered the car along the wrong lane.

"What are you doing!" she cried when a car approached from the opposite direction. "Stick to the right!"

"I thought you said left, Ma'am?" Bart inquired respectfully.

"Turn left but stay in your lane!"

He coughed deferentially as the other car zoomed past. It, too, was in the wrong lane. "Ma'am, in this country we drive on the left."

She uttered a startled little laugh. "Of course. I totally forgot."

"Good thing you're not driving, huh?" said Chase with a smile. He was rubbing her lower back and she was glad he was with her. Even if they struck out, she had to keep moving. If she just sat there on that couch she'd go nuts.

"We're approaching a crossroads, Ma'am," said the driver.

"Straight ahead," she said.

The driver didn't question her judgment. He simply did as he was told, which was a good thing, for she had absolutely no idea where she was going!

§.

Okay, so there was no way we could open that door from the inside, that much we'd ascertained. But how about the window? I pushed the button that operated the window and lo and behold! It inched down ever so slowly.

"Who's going to jump?" asked Harriet.

We were going pretty fast, and jumping now would probably get us killed. Unless we could aim ourselves onto the shoulder, into the high grass.

I glanced out the window, but all I could see was a guardrail.

Not the best landing spot for a sensitive cat.

"I'll go first," said Brutus bravely.

"In this country it is customary for women and children to go first," said Sweetie. She glanced at Harriet. "Which means we get to go first, then the prissy white cat, then the gray one and finally the fat, red cat."

"I'm not a woman," said Dooley.

"No, but you're a child," the corgi explained in a kindly tone.

"I'm not a child!" said Dooley.

"Fine, then you can go last," Sweetie snapped.

The corgi darted a peek out the window, saw that

guardrail, and retreated. "I'm not doing it," she announced. "Not a chance. That jump will end me."

The others seemed to agree, and darted expectant looks at me.

"You go, cat," said Molly. "You go and call the police."

"I'm not jumping," I said. "I'll break my neck."

"No, you won't. You're fat. All that blubber will act like a cushion."

"I'm not fat—I'm big-boned!"

"Of course you are," said Sweetie. "Now jump already, will you? Cats have nine lives, while we dogs only have one. So what if you get smushed? You'll still have eight lives left."

"Unless he's done this before," Fräulein pointed out. "In which case he'll only have seven lives left—or six."

"Six lives is better than none," Sweetie pointed out.

"It's a myth!" I said. "We don't have nine lives! If I die, that's the end!"

"Max!" said Brutus. "Never tell our deepest secrets to a dog!"

He was right. We don't spill the beans to dogs. Just like dogs will never open up to a cat about what makes them tick. It's not done, trust me. It might give the other species the upper hand and that's a big no-no in pet world.

"A collar," I said. "Quick. Someone give me a collar."

The corgis stared at me. "We're not giving you our collars," said Sweetie. "Do you have any idea how much these collars cost? This is gold plating, in case you didn't know."

"We're leaving a trail of breadcrumbs!" I said. "Quick. Before the doofus finds out the window is open!"

"Why don't you use your collar?" said Molly suspiciously.

"I don't have one!"

"See?" said Sweetie. "I told you they're street cats. Only street cats have no collars."

"Oh, for crying out loud," I grunted, then took a firm grip

on Sweetie's collar and yanked. Of course the thing didn't budge.

"Help!" she yelped. "He's gone mad! He's trying to kill me!"

"Oh, just give him the collar already," said Fräulein. She pressed a paw to her friend's collar and it clicked open. And as I swung it through the window, the driver glanced back, noticed the window was open, cursed and closed it.

I looked back at the collar, which was lying in the road. I just hoped Odelia would find it. Or else we were royally screwed.

CHAPTER 26

*O*delia and Chase were still in hot pursuit, even though Odelia had a hard time trusting her instincts. Every road she took had the potential of leading them further and further away from her cats and the corgis. On the other hand, it might lead them closer and closer to where they were taking them...

"Police will catch him," said Bart, as if he'd read her mind. "A network of sophisticated cameras covers a large part of the city. If he passes a camera they'll be able to track him. He's driving the Queen's car, so he won't get far."

"Doesn't the car have a tracking device?" asked Chase.

"It did. They took it out last year. The Queen's husband didn't like the idea of being tracked all the time. He likes to take the car for a spin, you see."

"Too bad," said Chase.

"It is," said Bart. "Then again, you have to respect a person for not wanting to be tracked. There is still such a thing as privacy in this country."

"Sometimes staying safe trumps privacy."

"The Queen and her husband are set in their ways, sir."

"She's going to be devastated if something happens to her corgis," said Odelia, biting her nails as her heart tapped a nervous pattern in her chest.

"Oh, yes," said Bart. "Sometimes I think she loves those animals more than her own family. Then again, I can't blame her. At least the corgis never give her any trouble."

"Have you ever driven the Duke and Duchess of Essex?"

"Can't say that I have, Ma'am. I have a friend who does, though."

She wondered how to formulate her next question.

"Any issues?" asked Chase, beating her to the punch.

She gave him a grateful nod.

"You mean, has something like this ever happened to them?"

"Uh-huh."

The driver thought for a moment. "Well, Fluffy was never kidnapped as far as I know. My friend did witness an incident shortly after they were married. A reporter who came to the house and made a big fuss about wanting to talk to the Duchess. He wasn't allowed to come anywhere near her, though."

"Who was he?"

"Well-known bloke. Otis Robbins? He does one of those morning shows. Personally I never watch him. Too full of himself. My mum loves him, though. She's a big fan."

"Why did he make a fuss?"

"I reckon he wanted to interview her for his show, and when she refused he blew his top. You can't just walk up to a royal and shove a camera in their face the way you can with regular folk on the street. He should have known that. Another fork in the road coming up, Ma'am."

She closed her eyes and was about to say left when Chase said, "Hey, isn't that a dog collar?"

The driver pulled over and Chase quickly got out. In the

middle of the road, a fancy dog collar lay. It was velvety red with a gold medallion.

When he brought it back to the car, he held it up. "Sweet-ie," he read.

"That's one of the Queen's corgis," said Bart excitedly. "Good catch, sir."

"So they definitely came this way," said Odelia. Her heart lifted and did a happy little dance. Her intuition wasn't leading them astray. Instead, it was leading them closer to her beloved pets.

"Let's keep going," said Chase. "Maybe we can catch up with them."

And as the car eased into traffic once more, Odelia found herself thinking about the driver's words. The reporter. Could he have something to do with this whole thing? Somehow she doubted it. Why would a reporter try to murder the Duchess? He could simply kill her with his sharp tongue.

࿔

The car was still zooming along the road, and I found myself thinking about Odelia. If I had to spend the rest of my life with this crook, I'd miss her very much. Odelia was the only human I'd ever owned, and so I didn't have a large frame of reference, but my instinct told me that I'd hit the jackpot when I'd landed on her doorstep. And that it could only go downhill from there.

"They'll probably sell us to the highest bidder," said Sweetie. "I wonder how much I will fetch."

"A thousand pounds," said Fräulein.

"A million, rather," said Sweetie.

"Maybe a billion!" Molly said.

"Maybe they'll sell us to someone in the Middle East," said Sweetie. "And he'll treat us like royalty."

"You're already treated like royalty," I said.

"Yes, but this time we'll be treated like oil sheik royalty, which is always a step up from those old and dusty European royals."

"I think the European royals are the best," said Fräulein. "New money simply can't compete with all that style and class."

"It can," said Sweetie. "They've been buying up so much of London soon they'll own the entire town, the Queen and all the other royals included."

"I miss Odelia," I announced, deciding to change the topic. I found all this talk of being sold off to the highest-bidding oil sheik frankly depressing.

"And I miss Gran," said Dooley.

"I miss Marge," said Harriet.

"I miss them all!" said Brutus, who possessed a sentimental streak I never even suspected he had.

"Oh, stop whining, you lot," said Sweetie. "You'll be adopted by a nice family, who'll feed you and give you plenty of cuddles."

"It's not the same," said Harriet.

"Yeah, you don't know our humans," Dooley chimed in. "They're the best."

"Look, it's not that I don't like the Queen," said Sweetie, "but mostly I like the lifestyle. You know? The best food, the best pillows, the best clothes, the best dog walkers... What I won't miss is the weather. London is so dreary."

"Oh, so dreary," said Molly with an eyeroll.

"The weather. Oh, don't get me started on the weather."

"Horrible weather. Simply ghastly."

"Some days I don't even want to get up."

"A lot of days."

"And then there's Dubai. Sunny and bright. My kind of place."

"My kind of place, too."

"Dubai is, like, a hundred degrees on a cold day," Fräulein pointed out.

"So? They have air-conditioning. It's all about the lifestyle."

"The lifestyle is the thing," Molly chimed in.

"Give me Buckingham Palace over some nondescript air-conditioned luxury condo in Dubai every day," said Fräulein.

"They probably don't even want you in Dubai," said Harriet, who seemed to have tired of the incessant inane jabbering. "Probably you'll be sold to someone living in some hellhole in the middle of nowhere."

"Like Chechnya," said Brutus with a smirk. "Or Moldova."

"Or maybe some African warlord will buy you so he can roast you over a slow fire and eat you," said Harriet. "And then he'll post the picture on Insta."

The three corgis stared at her, then Sweetie and Molly shook their heads, smiling indulgently. "Don't talk rubbish, cat," said Sweetie.

"Yeah, don't talk rubbish," Molly said.

"Why would anyone want to eat us?"

"Some people eat dogs," I said. "The Chinese, for instance. They consider dog meat a real treat."

Their smiles vanished and their eyes turned to the driver.

"Hey, Mr. Kidnapper!" Sweetie yelled. "You're not going to sell us to the Chinese, are you? Mr. Kidnapper!"

But the diver ignored them. He probably didn't speak dog.

Soon the car was slowing down, and then turned off the road, gravel crunching under the wheels until it pulled to a stop.

"I think we're there," said Sweetie. "I think this is it."

"Oh, I do hope it's Dubai and not China," said Molly breathlessly.

The window zipped down and a man looked in on us. I couldn't see his face, but I could tell he wasn't happy. Partly from the colorful curses he uttered and partly from the way he slammed his fist against the roof of the car, making us all jump up. "You've got to be kidding me!" he cried.

"Don't worry," said the driver. "I'll get rid of the cats."

"You took the wrong dogs!"

"No, I didn't."

"You took the Queen's corgis!"

"So?"

"You idiot! You were supposed to take Tessa's dog—not the Queen's!"

"Who cares? You told me to snatch royal dogs so I snatched royal dogs. And I'm throwing the cats in as a bonus. Except for the fat one. That's mine."

"Oh, for Christ's sakes. Take them back."

"Wait, what?"

"Don't you realize what you've done? The entire country will be looking for those dogs. And I don't even want to describe what they'll do to the man who took them. You, sir, are an idiot. A moron!"

"Hey! Sticks and stones, mate!"

The man was walking away.

"What about my money?!"

"Return those dogs!" the man yelled back. "Or you'll be sorry!"

"We had a deal!"

But the man got into his car and drove off.

"He wanted Fluffy," said Sweetie. "Can you believe it? He prefers a stupid mongrel over us!"

"Why would anyone want to steal Fluffy?" Harriet asked.

"Probably another Tessa-hater," I said. "Wanting to get back at her for some perceived slight or offense she caused."

But the corgis weren't listening. Instead, they were arguing the merits and demerits of Fluffy, whom they didn't seem to like all that much.

"So now what?" said the guy, glancing back at us.

"Better take us back," said Molly. "The Queen will be worried."

"I thought you didn't care about the Queen?" said Harriet.

"Oh, will you please shut up, cat?" said Sweetie imperiously.

"You know what?" said the kidnapper. "I'll just dump you here. The guy is probably right. Pretty soon Scotland Yard will be breathing down my neck."

And so he got out, slammed the door, and started jogging off!

He didn't get far, though, for a similar Range Rover to ours suddenly materialized, tires screeching as it pulled to a stop, then Chase jumped out! After a short chase, Chase tackled the guy and wrestled him to the ground.

"That's Chase!" cried Brutus. "That's my human!"

Odelia then came running in our direction, opened the door and, with tears in her eyes, said, "You guys—are you all right?"

And I have to admit I got a little teary, too, as we all jumped into her arms.

"Drama queens," said Sweetie.

"I think it's pretty sweet," said Fräulein.

CHAPTER 27

"*D*id you see the man's face?" asked Odelia.

Max shook his head. "I'm afraid I didn't."

The others all shook their heads, too. They hadn't seen the man either.

"What about the corgis?"

The corgis were being checked out by a doctor, but so far they seemed to be fine. The kidnapper, a low-level career criminal, had been contacted by the unknown man a couple of days ago. The scheme he proposed was simple: dress up like one of the royal drivers, and use any opportunity to kidnap the royal dog. Of course the crook had bungled the thing by kidnapping the corgis instead. He'd figured three royal dogs was better than one. Apparently not.

They were on a stretch of road very light on traffic, parked on the shoulder in the middle of nowhere. All around there was only greenery. No houses. No sign of civilization except for the asphalt, and the gravel of the shoulder.

She watched as Max approached the corgis, then returned a few moments later. "They are so hard to talk to," he said with a sigh. "Cocky, you know."

"Cocky corgis?" said Odelia with a grin. "That sounds like a book title."

"Well, anyway, Fräulein is not as cocky as her colleagues, and she claims the man looked familiar, though she doesn't know who he is, either."

"But she saw his face?"

"Briefly. They were sitting closer to him when he looked in on us."

"Did they describe him?"

"Medium height and build. Average features. Sweetie thinks he was blond, Fräulein claims he was brown, Molly swears he was black going on gray."

"You could ask a sketch artist," said Harriet. "You did that once before, remember?"

Odelia did remember, only she'd been home in Hampton Cove that time, and her uncle had officiated the proceedings. Gran had pretended to be the witness, while being fed information by the actual witness, a cat named Big Mac. This time it would be practically impossible to pull off the same stunt: the corgis would have to talk to Max, who'd have to translate, so she could describe the kidnapper to the sketch artist. And she couldn't even reasonably claim she'd actually seen the man, as they'd only arrived after he left.

"Sweetie did say he had a babyface, though Molly claims he had a long, thin face. They didn't notice eye color or any other particular details."

"An ordinary-looking man trying to abduct Tessa's dog," she said musingly.

"Could it be the same person who's been trying to kill her?" asked Brutus.

"Could be," she admitted.

"Aren't there any cameras around here?" asked Max.

She glanced around, and caught sight of Chase, who was still talking to the police. He was the hero of the hour. The man who'd taken down the kidnapper. "I doubt it," she said. Unless someone had fastened a camera to a tree. The kidnapper wasn't stupid. He picked this place for a reason.

Chase came jogging up. "It's in the hands of the police now," he said. "I'm sure they know what they're doing. They were surprised when I told them I'm a cop myself." He waved as the cop car sped by, the kidnapper in the back.

"That guy just became public enemy number one," said Odelia.

"He claims he doesn't know who the client was. He was contacted by text, and only met the guy for the first time today."

"So what did he look like, this mystery man?"

"Medium build, medium height, average face... He was wearing a ball cap to partially obscure his features."

"Hair color?"

"He figures the man was bald, hence the ball cap."

Odelia groaned in frustration. Four witnesses and four different descriptions.

"Let's get back to the cottage," said Chase. "We don't want to keep Her Royal Highness waiting."

The Queen, in a highly unusual initiative, had instructed Odelia and Chase to return her precious corgis. Apparently she didn't trust anyone at this point, and Chase and Odelia were, after all, highly regarded by Tessa and Dante.

The corgis had been checked out, and were returned to the Queen's Range Rover. This time Chase took the wheel, while Bart took the wheel of the second Rover, and together they drove back to the cottage, Chase following behind Bart, who knew the way—or had a good command of the royal GPS.

"I'm so glad he didn't sell us to the highest bidder," said Harriet from the backseat.

"I'm glad, too," said Odelia.

"He was going to keep Max," said Dooley. "He liked him because he's red and fat."

Odelia smiled. "Max isn't fat and he isn't red. He's big-boned and blorange. Isn't that right, Max?" When Max didn't respond, she looked over. The little guy had tears in his eyes. "Oh, sweetie," she said, and took him on her lap.

"I love you, Odelia," Max breathed, choking up.

"And I love you, sweetie," she said, and gave him a cuddle.

❧

"Oh, get a room," said Molly.

"Did she just call my name?" asked Sweetie.

"She said 'sweetie,' not 'Sweetie,'" said Fräulein.

"Did you tell your human this kidnapper guy was going to sell us to the ruler of Dubai?" asked Molly. "Which wouldn't have been all that bad."

"I think all's well that ends well," said Fräulein.

"I guess so," said Molly, a little dejected. Apparently she'd been looking forward to her Dubai adventure.

"You were never going to be sold to anyone," I said. "The kidnapper wanted to kidnap Fluffy as a way of getting back at Tessa."

"Such bad taste," said Sweetie, shaking her head at so much foolishness.

"Someone's been trying to hurt Tessa for days. And it's very well possible that they planned to use Fluffy to lure Tessa into a trap."

"Smart thinking, Max," said Odelia. "I hadn't thought of that."

"Was the Queen worried about us?" asked Molly.

I translated her words for Odelia's sake.

"The Queen was worried sick," she said.

"Oh," said Molly, and thought for a moment. "I like the

Queen," she said finally. "She's been very good to us over the years."

"She has," confirmed Sweetie. "I'm actually glad we weren't sold to Dubai."

"How about you, Odelia?" asked Dooley. "Did you miss us?"

She smiled. "Of course. I wouldn't have known what to do if something had happened to you. I love you guys so, so much."

The corgis were speechless. "Does she really mean that?" asked Sweetie.

I relayed the message and Odelia responded, "Of course. They're my babies."

"Mh," said Molly, as if she found it hard to believe anyone could care that much for a cat.

"I guess we learned a valuable lesson today," said Fräulein.

"What's that?" asked Sweetie.

"That you two knuckleheads are even dumber than I thought. And that humans love their cats, too."

"Thank you for coming to find us, Odelia," I said.

"Oh, Maxie," she said, and tickled my belly until ï fell off her lap laughing.

Even the corgis joined in at some point, proving that even snooty dogs can get unsnootied when pushed.

CHAPTER 28

They were all gathered in the war room—actually Dante and Tessa's office. Present were Dante, Tessa and Angela, Odelia, Chase and Gran, and Tessa's cousin Nesbit. The Queen had left with her entourage and her corgis, happy to return to the safety of Buckingham Palace. The events of the past few hours had shaken the monarch to the core, and it was obvious Dante and Tessa felt guilty about the whole thing. After all, the kidnapper had targeted Fluffy, and not the corgis.

"My grandmother is still convinced the kidnappers were targeting her corgis, and not Fluffy," said the Duke now. "There have been plots to kidnap them before, but this is the first time an attempt actually succeeded. Almost."

"Have they caught the guy who gave the kidnap order?" asked Odelia.

Tessa's cousin shook his head. "Not yet. They'll catch him sooner or later, though."

"No security cameras, right?" said Chase.

"None. They picked a great spot to skedaddle."

"Too bad the whole episode spooked the Queen," said

Gran. "We were really bonding there. Do you think the chances of her dropping by for another visit are high, medium or rare?"

"Non-existent," said Dante dryly. "She's never coming back here—at least not in the foreseeable future. Gran loves those corgis almost as much, or maybe even more, than her own offspring, so to return to the place where they were snatched is not going to hold a lot of appeal to her."

"Nuts," grumbled Gran, whose hopes of learning at the knee of the master had received a powerful blow.

"So let's discuss theories," said Tessa, getting back to the nub of the thing. She directed her next question to her cousin. "Who do you think is responsible for these attacks, Nesbit? What do your colleagues think?"

"My colleagues think most likely this is the work of a disgruntled employee." He took out a notebook. "I've compiled a list of all the people who've worked for you, past and present. One of them must be behind this whole thing. I've cross-referenced with the people present at the Summer Show, the homeless shelter, and of course here at the house. When the tea incident happened, Suzy was there, and so were your cook Carolyn and personal assistant Sherri. At the Summer Show, Sherri was present, but she wasn't at the homeless shelter and neither was Carolyn. Only Suzy was there."

"There are others," said Tessa, and brought out her phone. "I've compiled my own list of people who seem to resent me to the extent they might want to harm me." She cleared her throat and gave her husband a weary look. "You're not going to like this, Dante."

"I think I can take it," said the Duke.

"Your brother and his wife, your friend Damien and his cronies. And of course your ex-girlfriends Chrissie, Missy and Sissy. None of them like me very much, and all of them have expressed, veiled or unveiled, the notion that I stole you away from them, which makes me their mortal enemy."

"That's ludicrous," said Dante. "I broke up with them a long time ago. When we met I'd been single for months."

"Still. They hate my guts, and so do your brother and his wife."

"Nonsense. Jennie and Jeremy adore you."

"Yeah, right. That's why they referred to me as 'that horrible woman' at your aunt Caroline's reception last month. I happened to overhear them."

"Well, you must have heard wrong."

"Don't forget your grandmother, Dante," said Angela. "I know Tessa is too kind to mention her but she's definitely on my list of suspects."

"My grandmother? Really, Angela?"

"The Queen is notoriously averse to scandal. A divorce is the last thing she wants, so if she were to get rid of Tessa the only option would be to make it look like an accident. She could have put someone on staff here to do the dirty work," she added when Dante made protesting noises.

"Nonsense. My gran has been nothing but supportive of Tessa from the first. In fact she's told me on more than one occasion how happy she is that I finally found a life partner. She was worried before, and is over the moon now. Especially after the birth of Silvy. She absolutely adores her great-grandchild."

"So what about this Damien character?" asked Chase.

Dante hesitated. "Damien is... disappointed that I'm not the friend I used to be. And of course he blames Tessa to some extent, but in equal measure he blames me. Deep down, though, I think he knows that change is inevitable, and that he can't expect the father of a newborn to hit the clubs hard every night. He also knows he has to settle down himself eventually, and he's rebelling. He would never harm Tessa. I vouch for the bloke. He's a good egg."

"So that leaves us with…" Odelia consulted her own list. "You haven't mentioned the nanny yet."

"She wasn't anywhere near the Summer Show, or the homeless shelter," said Nesbit. "She also wasn't at the house when the tea thing happened. She'd gone home."

"What about the housekeeper?" Odelia remembered she'd kicked out her cats the night before, which of course didn't mean she was a killer, but still.

"She was here when the tea incident happened, but she didn't attend the Summer Show, and she wasn't at the homeless shelter this morning."

"So where does that leave us?" asked Angela.

"Nowhere," said Gran.

Tessa threw up her hands. "This is crazy. Someone is trying to kill me and we're just going around in circles. This person might very well be on the verge of striking again and we're simply getting nowhere."

"Have you examined the bullet that grazed Tessa's cheek?" asked Chase.

"We have—in all discretion. It was fired from a Glock 17, probably procured on the black market, as ownership of handguns is tightly regulated."

"I think we should let the police handle things from now on," said Dante, voicing an opinion he'd expressed before. "All this cloak and dagger stuff is all very exciting, but they have the resources and the experience to handle the investigation the way it should have been handled from the start."

"You seem to forget that all members of our protection team are police officers," said Tessa. "They're more than qualified to deal with this."

"After three botched attempts on your life and one dognapping excuse me if I have my doubts about their professionalism, Tessa. I think they should all go and be replaced by an entirely new team. No offense, Nesbit."

"None taken," said Odelia's cousin. "They're good guys, all of them, dedicated to your family, but whoever is behind this is a slippery bastard."

"Give us one more chance," said Odelia. "I know we can find this guy."

Dante wavered, but Tessa was giving him a pleading look and finally he relented. "All right, fine. One more day. But if by tomorrow evening you don't have a solid lead, I'm bringing Scotland Yard into the picture. This has got to stop, Tessa. I won't let you put yourself in harm's way like this."

"Odelia will find out what's going on," said Tessa, with a conviction Odelia herself wasn't feeling.

One more day. She needed to get her act together and get to the bottom of this thing or else they were all on the next plane back to Hampton Cove, or worse, the next attempt on Tessa's life would be successful. And she would never forgive herself if that happened.

A child started crying in the next room, and Tessa got up. She placed a hand on Odelia's shoulder. "I trust you, Odelia. You can do this."

If only she felt as confident in her abilities as Tessa did…

CHAPTER 29

While the humans were all ensconced in a room discussing the recent dramatic events, I was wandering the house and wondering how to contribute to the unraveling of the mystery. Frankly I didn't have a lot to contribute. As far as I could tell anyone could have kidnapped us. And it wasn't anyone we'd met so far.

So I decided to give the investigation a rest for now, and await further instructions from sleuth-in-charge Odelia.

And as I was pottering to and fro, trying to find that perfect spot to take a well-deserved nap, I was softly humming a little tune to myself. It's my habit to sing, not when I'm in the shower, for as you may or may not know, cats don't enjoy taking showers, but to aid the thinking process. Also, I'm something of a songbird. What can I say—I just enjoy the joy of singing!

Dooley, who was sampling a spot on the couch in front of the big television set, winced as I passed and sang my few bars.

Harriet, who was inspecting a nice throw pillow on the second couch, likewise screwed up her face and gave me a long, lingering look that didn't harbor a lot of warmth and appreciation for livening up her day with song.

Brutus, who was eyeing a shelf laden with knickknacks, thinking up ways and means of making the jump and lounging there for a while, shook his head. "Can you please stop that racket? I can't hear myself think."

"It is a little annoying," agreed Fluffy, who, as queen of the castle, had reserved the prime spot all to herself: a basket on the floor near the window, where she had a great overview both of the goings-on inside and outside.

"I was just humming a gay little tune," I said defensively.

"We need to continue our lessons, Max," Harriet said now. "And we might as well do it now, as there seems to be a lull in the investigation."

A lull was right. It would appear that none of the humans had a clue how to proceed in catching this dastardly demon who was gunning for lovely Tessa.

"Oh, great," I said, not expecting this. "I would love to put in some more practice."

That way, when we finally got back from our trip overseas, I could be reinstated as a full-blown and appreciated member of cat choir once more. Maybe I could even induce Shanille to let me sing a solo. Singing solos, it would appear, is what being part of a choir is all about: it lends one prestige and makes one the standard-bearer of the group, if one catches my meaning.

"Where do you want me to sit?" I asked. "Near the window? Or maybe higher? For the acoustics," I clarified. "It's very important to have great acoustics when you're singing. It gives it that little extra oomph your musical aficionado wants."

"I think your voice has all the oomph it needs," said Brutus. He'd finally decided against jumping on top of the high shelf. A wise decision, I thought, as those little knickknacks contained a framed picture of Silvy and a portrait of the Queen, and if Brutus knocked them all to the floor, there would be hell to pay, or at least a stern rebuke from the Duke.

"Maybe we should take this outside," said Harriet after careful consideration. "There are too many sensitive ears in here to be subjected to the kind of racket you call singing. I'm thinking about the baby."

I should probably have felt insulted but strangely enough I wasn't. I was touched that Harriet would want to protect me from the ire of the humans. Most of them are, after all, cultural barbarians, everybody knows that. So I tripped to the door, only to find it closed again, with no pet flap in sight.

"So how do we get out of here?" I asked Fluffy, lounging languorously in her pillow-covered basket.

"You have to ask one of the humans," she said. "I usually yap loudly, and that does the trick. If that doesn't work, I jump up and down someone's leg."

I wasn't going to lower myself to jumping up and down someone's leg. Cats are better than that. But the meowing could work. So I licked my lips, opened my mouth, and let my larynx do the talking. And when that didn't produce results, Harriet, Brutus and Dooley joined in for an impromptu recital.

"It helps if you stand in front of the door," Fluffy advised. "That way they know exactly what you want."

We all moved to the door and restarted our mini-concert for an audience of one: Fluffy, who was holding her paws to her ears, grimacing generously.

I guess dogs are cultural barbarians, too.

The meeting was still in full swing, so those inside couldn't be bothered with our plight. Luckily there's always staff members and security people flitting about a royal home like this, and one of them now stuck her head around a corner. I recognized her as Suzy, the maid. When she saw what was going on, she approached hesitantly.

"Um... I guess you want to go out, right?"

We all meowed in confirmation, happy at her acumen.

"The thing is, I'm not sure if I'm allowed to open the door. What with the whole kidnapping thing and all."

We meowed a little louder, singing with panache and vigor.

"Nature calls, lady," said Brutus. "And if you don't let us out right now, we won't be held responsible for the consequences, if you know what I mean."

"He means we're going to leave a permanent mark on the floor," I said.

"Oh, dear," said Suzy, bringing a hesitant hand to her face. "Don't you have, um, litter boxes to do your business in?"

"We do, but we're rough-and-tumble cats," Brutus continued the negotiations. "We like to do it in the bushes."

"I guess you really need to go, huh?" she said finally, darting uncertain glances in the direction of the office. "Oh, I guess it's fine," she said, convincing herself. "Just don't tell anyone it was me that let you out, all right?" Then she laughed. "How silly of me. Who are you going to tell? You're just cats. You can't talk."

So she opened the door. Outside, a burly guard turned his head.

"It's all right, Phil," she said. "It's just the cats wanting to go for a walk."

"Of course," said Phil with an indulgent smile. "We don't want those precious little furballs to do their business on the couch, do we?"

"No, we don't," Suzy said a little shyly.

"So how are things with you, Suzy?"

"Oh, can't complain," Suzy said conversationally. "This

kidnapping thing has got us all on edge, though. Who would do such a horrible thing?"

"The world is full of monsters, Suzy," he said indulgently. "Which is why it's good to have a guy like me around, to protect you and yours."

"And I'm ever so glad for that, Phil," she said with a little giggle.

We decided to let the two lovebirds explore their budding affair, and moved off into the wild—or at least the perfectly sculpted gardens that surrounded the cottage.

There were no other humans in sight, not even a pesky reporter trying to snap Tessa's picture, and I breathed a sigh of relief. I hadn't realized it before, but the atmosphere inside the house was rife with tension. So it felt great to be away from that for a moment.

"I'll bet Harriet is going to make a great singer out of you yet, Max," said Dooley encouragingly.

"Thanks, Dooley," I said. "I certainly hope so."

"When I'm through with you, you'll be ready to sing at the Royal Albert Hall," said Harriet.

"What's the Royal Albert Hall?" asked Dooley.

"It's like Madison Square Garden, only British. And royal, obviously. You're going to turn heads, Max. Just you wait and see."

"Max doesn't need to turn heads," said Brutus. "He just has to open his mouth." And he gave me what I thought was a very insensitive grin.

"I'm at a very difficult time in my life right now, Brutus," I said. "I'm feeling vulnerable, and it wouldn't hurt for you to give me some much-needed encouragement."

"You mean you're traumatized, Max?" asked Dooley.

"I think there's every chance that I am," I said. "Being ridiculed for wanting to be a better singer is the stuff of trauma."

"You need a shrink," said Brutus.

I shivered. The last time shrinks were mentioned was when Brutus was having doubts about his sexual orientation. He'd suddenly gotten it into his nut that he might be a female deep down inside. Luckily the moment had passed, and now he was his usual obnoxious self again.

"Okay, let's get this show on the road," said Harriet, clapping her paws.

We'd found a nice little clearing behind the cottage, where we wouldn't be disturbed and where we wouldn't disturb anyone either.

"Now simply repeat after me, Max," said Harriet, and started singing a nice, simple scale. "La la la la la la la la laaaah. Now you."

"Lar lar lar lar laaaaar laaaaar lar laaaaaaaarrrrrrrrr," I warbled.

Harriet pressed her paws to her ears, and so did Brutus and Dooley.

Mh. Looked like I wasn't ready for the Royal Albert Hall yet.

CHAPTER 30

The meeting was over and the participants all walked out of Tessa's office. And as they did, Nesbit fell into step beside Odelia and said, "There's something I've been meaning to tell you, Odelia, if you have a moment."

"Yes?" she said encouragingly. She liked the young security man. To come to his cousin's aid like this meant a lot to Tessa, especially as the rest of her family had behaved a little despicably towards her in recent months.

"It's probably nothing, which is why I didn't want to bring it up in there," he said apologetically. "But I found this."

He handed her his tablet. "What am I looking at?"

"It's a letter from a reader. Posted when Tessa and Dante had just started dating. It was posted in *The Sun*, the UK's biggest tabloid."

She quickly read the letter. 'It's outrageous that a foreigner like Tessa Torrance can just come in and sweep our prince off his feet. Aren't there enough nice English girls? Why an American? I can promise you this, Dante: the people won't forgive you. They'll do whatever they can to break up this match made in hell. I know I will.' Signed, 'A concerned English rose.'

She looked up, and Nesbit gave her a meaningful look.

"So who is this English rose?" she asked.

"That's just it, one of the editors came forward after he heard about the kidnap attempt. This so-called English rose wrote a bunch of these letters. One of them threatening Tess's dog. She seemed to take umbrage to the fact that Tessa brought her dog Fluffy to England. Said there are plenty of perfectly good dogs right here and she shouldn't have brought in an American bitch."

"Nice. So who is she?"

"Suzy Boots."

"Suzy wrote this?" asked Odelia, shocked.

"Apparently. And about a thousand comments like this. She's very active. What some people would call a troll. I searched some more, and found that she comments freely on her Facebook page, too. And that she's left hundreds of comments on Dante and Tess's Instagram. All of it extremely vitriolic."

He scrolled through a few of the comments from Suzy's Facebook page. 'The Duchess of Essex is a classless gold digger,' was one of the nicer ones.

"And here's the clincher," he said.

'I happen to work for Tessa,' she'd written in response to a comment by someone else, 'so I know what she's like as a person. And while I agree with you that we should give her a chance, I've given her plenty of chances, and she's let me down every single time. The woman is a fungus to be got rid of.'

"We need to talk to her," said Odelia. "Right now."

"She could simply be one of those poison pen people."

"She posted threats, Nesbit. Actual threats. Why didn't you tell Tessa?"

He mussed up his hair, looking sheepish. "She's in such a state—I didn't want to make it worse by bothering her with unfounded accusations against a member of her staff. Which is why I decided to run it by you first."

"You did well," she said, giving his arm a grateful squeeze. "But I think this is a genuine threat, and Tessa needs to know." She took the tablet and looked around for Tessa. She found her in the nursery, cradling Silvy. "There's something you need to see, Tessa," she said, handing her Nesbit's tablet.

When Tessa was confronted with the evidence, her expression darkened. "I think we just found our assailant."

"Where is she?" asked Odelia.

"Cleaning," said Tessa curtly.

Dante, who'd noticed something was going on, joined them. Without a word, Tessa handed him the tablet. As he read the comments, his eyes went wide. "Suzy wrote this?"

"This and a whole lot more," said Odelia.

"See!" he cried. "I told you to put in stricter background checks!"

"This is not the time for 'I told you so's,' Dante," she said, stalking off. The others all followed her into the living space. "Suzy!" she snapped when she caught up with the maid, who was turning down the bed in Gran's room.

"Yes, Ma'am?" said Suzy deferentially. She looked as mousy and reticent as ever. Hard to imagine she wrote the kind of stuff she did, Odelia thought.

"What's going on?" asked Chase, attracted by the sound of shouting voices.

"I think we've found our guy, and it's a girl," said Odelia.

"Suzy? Impossible," said Chase.

Suzy, who'd been handed the tablet, had turned as white as the sheets in her hand.

"Why did you do it?" demanded Tessa.

"I—I don't know," she stammered.

"It's obvious you hate my guts," said Tessa. "So why work for me?"

"I just figured—I..." She broke down in tears, but Tessa wasn't placated.

She took her by the arms and shook her. "You're the one who's been trying to kill me, aren't you? Answer me, dammit!"

The girl's eyes went wide. "Kill you? No, I swear I would never—"

"Of course you would. It's obvious from the stuff you wrote that you hate me so much you wouldn't hesitate to take matters into your own hands."

"No, I would never do you harm, Ma'am—never. For the baby and... and the Duke..." She directed a shy look at Dante, whom she obviously idolized.

"Oh, don't give me that bullshit. You decided to come and work for me so you could remove me from the equation and save Dante and the country."

"It's true that I was very upset when you and the Duke first started dating. And it's true I wrote all these things. But I've since changed my mind. Now that I've met you in person, I can see how wrong I was. How kind you are. And how good you are to the Duke and how much he loves you. And since the baby was born, I think you're the most wonderful mother and..."

"These comments—they were all written on your Face-book," said Tessa. "They paint a completely different picture. A very hateful, disgusting picture."

"I wrote those comments a long time ago. Since I started working for you I've stopped writing them—I swear," she said, directing her words to Dante.

"You wrote at least one comment after you started working here," said Odelia.

"I'm so sorry," she said, hanging her head. "I-I didn't know the Duchess the way I do now. I'm so ashamed of myself. I-I feel like…" She gulped. "I almost feel as if a different person wrote all these things. Not the real me but someone else entirely."

"You tried to kill my wife, Suzy," said Dante. "You have to understand there will be consequences. That we have to hand you over to the police now."

"But I didn't do it! I would never—"

"I'm very disappointed in you, Suzy. I really am."

"But sir!" she cried, tears springing to her eyes.

Odelia almost felt sorry for the girl. She was obviously delusional, to write the stuff she had—to do the things she did. She was also an accomplished liar.

"We can't involve the police," said Tessa. "It will create the biggest fuss."

"We have to, sweet pea," he said. "She needs to be punished to the full extent of the law, and that's something we can't do ourselves." He smiled as he tucked a strand of hair behind her ear. "Or did you think I was going to play judge, jury and executioner and sentence her all by myself?"

"No, of course not. I just…"

"This isn't the Middle Ages, darling. We don't lock people up in the Tower anymore. We let the police handle things—and the justice system. We're citizens of this country, just like every other person."

Tessa nodded. "Of course." She then directed a look of relief at Odelia. "You got her. You finally got her."

"Actually your cousin did," said Odelia. "Your real cousin."

Tessa threw herself into Nesbit's arms and the big guy actually blushed.

"It's over," said Angela with a smile. "It's really over."

It was, and Odelia sighed with relief. The ordeal was finally over.

CHAPTER 31

I was just about to break into song again, on Harriet's instigation, when voices drifted in our direction, interrupting my practice session.

"This place is infested with humans," Brutus grumbled, quite harshly I thought. After all, humans have a right to walk around free and untethered.

"England is a lot smaller than America," Harriet said. "Which is probably why there are humans everywhere."

She was right. Even though Hampton Cove isn't exactly the countryside, it's much more peaceful than the parts of England I'd seen so far.

"There are quiet parts," said Dooley now, much to my surprise. "In fact there are whole swaths of countryside where not a single person lives."

"And how would you know?" scoffed Brutus.

"I've seen it on TV," Dooley said. "Marge had a British kick for a while, and watched all things British. Crime shows, the news, and a show called *Countryfile* where they show the countryside. It's quite beautiful."

"Quite," Brutus mimicked with an eyeroll.

"No, it is. Very green, with pretty little villages dotting the rolling hills."

"Sounds like you wouldn't mind living there," I said.

He shrugged. "I'll live wherever my humans live. I'm easy that way."

I was the same way. If my human decided to move to Antarctica, I'd probably move there, too. Though I'd really prefer if she didn't. I don't like the cold all that much. Or the heat, for that matter. I guess I'm fussy that way.

The male voice drifted closer, and so Harriet decided to press pause on our practice session for the time being. She didn't want to spook people, she said.

I wondered if I should feel insulted but a man had come walking into the clearing, talking into his phone.

I immediately recognized him as the reporter who'd created such a fuss the night before, insisting he had every right to take pictures of Tessa and the baby. He put his phone away and lit up a cigarette. I had the impression he was waiting for someone.

"Isn't that the reporter from last night?" asked Harriet.

"Yup, that's him," I said.

"I don't like him," said Dooley.

"I don't like him either."

"What is he doing here? I thought he was told to stay away?" said Brutus.

"Looks like he's meeting someone."

"This should be interesting," said Harriet.

"I wonder who he's here to meet," said Dooley.

"Probably someone who works at the cottage," I said.

"But why?"

"Oh, Dooley, isn't it obvious?" said Harriet.

"No, it's not."

"He's a reporter, dying to write a juicy story about Tessa and Dante. And if he can't get near the cottage himself, either to interview them or to snap pictures, he needs other people to do it for him. And what better person than someone working there?"

"Um..." said Dooley, clearly not following.

"Someone who works for Tessa and Dante. Someone who can dish the dirt."

"Can't wait to see who the rat is," grunted Brutus.

"Rats!" Dooley cried, jumping a foot in the air.

"He means the informant," I said. "Not an actual rat."

"An informant ratting out his employers," Brutus grumbled. "Sounds like a rat to me."

So we waited patiently for the rat who was ratting out Tessa to show up, so we could rat the rat out to Tessa ourselves.

Unfortunately, I was so much in the swing of my rehearsal thing, that inadvertently I'd started doing those runs again. "Lar lar lar lar lar lar laaaaaaaaaar!" I sang quietly. Or at least I thought I was being quiet. Apparently I was mistaken, for the reporter glanced over as if stung.

When he spotted us, he growled, "I don't believe this— stupid cats!"

It would appear the man was not a cat person, for he picked up a dead branch from the ground and came charging in our direction—yelling some very unpleasant and rude words in the process!

Harriet zipped into the shrubbery, along with Dooley, but Brutus and I weren't that smart. Instead, we scooted up a tree and soon were ensconced on the highest branch, where the reporter couldn't reach us.

"And stay there!" he yelled, then walked away, shaking his head and muttering dark oaths under his breath.

It was only then that I realized the predicament we were in: we were thirty feet up from the ground, with no way to backtrack and get down again! And no friendly human in sight who could lend us a helping hand—or a pole!

"Um, Max," said Brutus, anxiously looking down at the ground below. "We're in trouble here, buddy."

"You don't say!" I said.

"Well, I did say. Just now."

"I know!"

"So why did you say 'You don't say?'"

"It's an expression!"

"Great. We're stuck in a tree and you have to go all grammar Nazi on me."

"Look, we're fine," I said as much for my own reassurance as his. "We're perfectly fine."

"Define fine."

"Harriet and Dooley will go and fetch Odelia and she will figure this out."

Brutus glanced down again. Harriet and Dooley were nowhere in sight.

"If Dooley lays one paw on my girl," he growled, "I'll rip his throat out."

"This is not the time to entertain your petty jealousies, Brutus," I said.

"It's not petty when it's real. They're in those bushes down there, and they're not coming out. I'll bet he's holding her, lending aid and comfort."

"So what's wrong with lending aid and comfort?"

"When I'm ripping his throat out he'll know what's wrong."

"Please control those primitive urges of yours, Brutus. What are we? Animals?"

"It's feline nature, Max! Cats thrown together tend to develop certain... feelings."

"Nonsense."

"Is it? What about Tom Hanks and his friend Wilson?"

"That was a volleyball."

"It still proves my point."

"Well, we've been thrown together in a dangerous situation," I told him. "And we're not developing certain feelings, are we?" Except extreme irritation.

"We're not a male and a female, Max. We can be cool with each other."

"Look, Dooley would never—"

"Oh, Dooley would most definitely jump at the chance to put his paws on Harriet. He's been praying for an opportunity to be alone with her in a situation where she's vulnerable and prone to errors of judgment! And all because of some dumb reporter who likes stalking innocent women and children!"

"Well, if you put it that way," I murmured.

We sat there for a moment, contemplating ways and means of getting out of the tree without risking our necks, but I couldn't come up with anything other than that our fate rested in the hands of Dooley and Harriet who still hadn't— at the time of writing—left those darn bushes!

"If I survive this I'm going to kill Dooley," said Brutus.

I didn't respond. I was starting to wonder how long the feline body can survive without taking nourishment and drink. Not long, I imagined.

And as the thought entered my mind, already my stomach was rumbling.

Yep, we were two dead cats, and all because of one cat-hating reporter and Dooley's out-of-control libido.

CHAPTER 32

*G*ran wasn't having a lot of fun. She'd come on this trip hoping it would be a blast, but so far it was more of a bust than a blast. The investigation was one of those weird ones, where you just kept going around in circles, and frankly she'd lost interest in the case the moment Odelia and Chase had taken the lead, making it clear they did not need a little old lady cramping their style.

And then there was the whole debacle with the Queen. Gran had hoped the Queen would become her BFF. That they'd exchange phone numbers and chat for hours and hours about their lives and how much they had in common. Instead, the Queen had been out of there like a flash the moment her precious corgis were returned, and she hadn't seen or heard from the woman since.

Not exactly the behavior of a true BFF.

She also hated the whole lockdown scenario they'd been living. She'd hoped to visit London and take in some of the sights—preferably with her new BFF by her side—but being locked in the cottage had put a stop to that.

So no trips to London. No invitations for a slumber party

at Buckingham Palace where she could have pillow fights with the Queen and drink hot cocoa while they swapped war stories from their long and eventful lives.

And now it seemed as if the whole thing was over before it even got started, with this maid being arrested. Talk about an anticlimax. The cops had dropped by and escorted the hate-spewing online troll into a car and had carted her off to prison and that was that. The end of the investigation and the end of their English sojourn. Soon it would be bye-bye and back to America.

She needed some air, that's what she needed. So she headed for the door and walked out. Some security guy was lounging out there, looking all threatening and bearded, but she just said, "I'm going for a walk," in a tone that allowed no backchat, and he merely nodded and watched her walk off.

He'd probably received instructions to protect Tessa, Dante and the baby, and those American tourists were all expendable. So if someone kidnapped them, who cared? Not Tessa—and most definitely not the Queen!

"Dumbasses," she muttered as she kicked a rock that had the gall to traverse her path.

She headed along a dirt road, and as she walked, soon her mood started improving considerably. It was a beautiful day, with the sun streaming through the canopy of leaves over-head and lovingly dappling the path ahead. Soon she was wondering if maybe they couldn't extend their trip for a couple of days. They'd probably only be in England this one time, and they needed to take advantage of the opportunity.

And she'd walked about half a mile when she was greeted by a surprising sight: Dooley and Harriet were hurrying down the road, and when they saw her, they practically yipped with joy.

"Thank God!" said Harriet. "Max and Brutus are in trouble, Gran!"

"What trouble?" she asked as she bent down, ignoring the ache in her back and the twin crackling sounds emanating from her creaky knees.

"They were chased up a tree by that nasty reporter and now they can't get down!" said Dooley, panting freely.

"Oh, heck," she said, straightening. "Show me the way, will ya?"

They showed her the way, and soon she found herself in a clearing, a faint whiff of cigarette smoke lingering in the air, probably from that nasty reporter, and when she looked up, she saw two cats, hugging a tree branch, and looking down at her with visible joy.

"Gran! Are we glad to see you!" Max shouted.

"Did you do hanky-panky with my girlfriend?!" Brutus demanded.

"Hanky-panky with your girlfriend? Are you nuts? There's only one person I'd do hanky-panky with and that's a prince. Unfortunately they're all taken, as far as I can tell. I'd settle for a duke or a count, but same story."

"I'm talking to Dooley," said Brutus, clearly delusional from being up in that tree.

"Brutus, you're an idiot!" Harriet shouted.

"Tell me the truth! Did he jump your bones when you were in those bushes?"

"Of course he didn't jump my bones!"

"You were in there an awfully long time!"

"We were hiding from that nutjob reporter!"

"That nutjob reporter is long gone!"

"Dooley kept saying we should hide out a little longer."

"A-ha! I knew it!"

"I thought he was still out there!" Dooley explained. "I could hear him. Breathing heavy and uttering threatening curses."

"That was Brutus you heard, Dooley," said Max.

"You jumped Harriet's bones, admit it!" Brutus shouted.

"No, I didn't!" Dooley shouted back.

"Oh, you're almost as bad as my boyfriends," said Gran. "Dumb as rocks."

"Can you please get us out of this tree, Gran?" asked Max.

"Do you want me to break my neck? Lemme go get some hero to fish you out of that damn tree. And next time use your heads before you pull a stunt like that."

"Don't leave us!" Brutus yelled, his plight suddenly more pressing than his petty jealousies.

"Don't worry!" she yelled. "I'll be back!"

She hurried back to the cottage, where the same burly guard cocked an eyebrow. "Had a nice walk, Ma'am?"

"My cats are stuck in a tree. Can you get them down?"

"I'm sorry, Ma'am. I can't leave my post."

"Oh, for crying out loud," she said, and headed into the house.

"My cats are stuck in a tree," she told Dante, who was pacing the living room. "Can you get them out?"

"What are you talking about?" he said, none too friendly, she thought.

Oh, had everyone lost their damn minds? "My cats!" she yelled, figuring all that inbreeding had turned the moron deaf. "They're stuck! In a tree!"

When he simply stared at her, she threw up her arms. She was starting to see that being queen wasn't all it was cracked up to be. The woman's grandson was obviously a brainless boob, her other grandson an even bigger numbskull, and the rest of the family probably wasn't any better. No wonder she preferred the company of a bunch of dogs over her nearest and dearest.

There was only man who could help her. One man in the whole universe. And it wasn't Superman, or Batman, or Spiderman or any of those chumps.

"Chase!" she screamed at the top of her lungs. "Chase Kingsley!"

The man of the hour arrived, looking cool as a cucumber as usual.

"Gran?" he said. "What's wrong?"

"It's Max and Brutus," she said. "They're stuck in a tree. Can you…"

He held up a hand. "Say no more."

Odelia now also came walking in from her bedroom. "What's going on?"

"The cats need saving," said Chase.

A resolute look stole over Odelia's face. "Lead the way," she said.

And Gran led the way. On the walk over, she explained the predicament, including the horrible role played by that vile reporter. When they arrived in the clearing, Max and Brutus were now clinging to each other, looking scared.

Chase put his hands to his mouth to form a makeshift megaphone and shouted, "Max! Brutus! Hang on! I'm coming to get you!"

"Yes, please, Chase!" Max yelled, a quiver in his voice.

"Oh, please, Chase!" Brutus said, a similar quiver in his voice.

Obviously the black cat had been chastened by his stay in the tree.

And before Gran and Odelia's eyes, not to mention Harriet and Dooley, Chase climbed that tree as if he'd never done anything else in his life.

"Be careful, honey," said Odelia, nervously biting her lip.

"Be back in a jiffy," the hero cop announced.

And he was. He climbed that tree as if it was the board-walk, transferred the two cats onto his broad shoulders, and then came climbing down again.

"Damn," said Gran when he placed Brutus in her arms

and Max in Odelia's. "You are something else, Chase, and I don't say that lightly."

"Oh, honey, you're a hero," said Odelia.

Max and Brutus, who were staring at the man adoringly, were too emotional for speech, but Dooley said it best when he spoke those historic words: "Chase is the greatest thing to hit this family since sliced bread."

CHAPTER 33

hat night, after everyone retired for the night, Gran was the only one still up. She looked a little sad, I thought, which worried me. She was on the sofa, channel-surfing and sipping from a glass of sherry, the sound of the TV muted so as not to disturb the rest of the house, with only Dooley and I to keep her company. Harriet and Brutus had had a reconciliation, and were somewhere outside, frolicking like a couple of frolicking honeymooners.

"What's wrong, Gran?" I asked after she'd been watching a man with big ears trying to teach a cat to jump through hoops. "Aren't you feeling well?"

"If you must know, I'm sad, Max," she said.

"Sad? But why? Suzy's been caught. Tessa is safe, and all's well that ends well."

"That's just it. All's well that ends well but no thanks to me—as usual. It seems to me that other people are always the hero and I'm the wild card."

"The wild card?"

"The fool. The silly sidekick who gets the funniest lines

171

but plays a minor part. I thought coming to England I could be the hero for once, you know."

"I thought you wanted to be queen?"

"That was just an idea. I should have known it wasn't gonna fly. Oh, why do I get these crazy ideas and then create trouble for everyone around me?"

"I like your ideas," said Dooley. "I think they're great. And how boring would life be if you weren't around to lend it some color and some fun?"

Gran smiled at these words and stroked Dooley's fur. "Sweet, sweet Dooley. What would I do without you guys?"

"I think Dooley is right," I said. "You're the heart of this family, Gran. You're its center. You're the glue that keeps the whole thing together."

"That's very kind of you to say, Max, but you know that's not true. I'm the fool. The court jester. Someone to make people laugh. The only reason they tolerate me is because I'm old and they can't get rid of me that easy."

"Everybody loves you, Gran," I said. "You're a real hoot."

"A real hoot," she repeated. "Yeah, that wasn't exactly my goal in life." She'd switched the channel again, and now a reporter was launching into some diatribe about Tessa. He was behind a desk and looked very serious and very angry. I sat up a little straighter when I recognized him. It was that same reporter again. The one who'd chased us up that tree that afternoon.

"Nasty piece of journalist," said Gran, shaking her head.

"He's not really a journalist," said Dooley. "He's a hate-monger and a troublemaker. At least that's what Dante said."

Gran smiled. "Hatemonger. That's a big word for you, Dooley."

"Thanks, Gran." He grinned, happy with the compliment.

I was listening intently to the reporter. His voice sounded

familiar, though I couldn't place it. Of course I'd heard him before, so that was probably it.

Next to Gran, a phone started singing out a tune. She frowned and picked it up. "The Duchess of Essex's phone. Who dis?"

When the voice on the other end replied something, her brow unfurrowed and shot into her curly white fringe. She sat up with a jerk.

"Your Royal Highness!" she cried.

"It's the Queen!" said Dooley.

"No, Tessa's gone to bed. Dante, too. The corgis? What about the corgis?"

She messed with the phone for a moment, and then suddenly we could both hear and see the Queen. Apparently she was using an app.

"Oh, Vesta. I'm so glad it's you," said the Queen. "I felt ever so silly calling Tessa, but I didn't know who else to call. But I'm so happy you picked up. I'm not sure she would have understood. It's the corgis, you see. They've been acting up. I think they saw something on the telly just now and they're suddenly all excited and yapping up a storm!"

"Put them on," said Gran firmly.

"Put them—what do you—"

"Trust me—just put them on," repeated Gran.

The corgis came into view, all three of them, seated on the couch, just like we were, and yapping excitedly when they caught sight of us.

"It's the guy!" said Sweetie.

"What guy?" I asked.

"The kidnapper!"

"They're saying it's the guy," I told Gran.

"Can you direct the camera at the TV, Your Majesty?" asked Gran.

"Oh, do call me Lizzie, please."

"Show us what's on TV, Lizzie."

"Will do," said Lizzie. She directed the camera at the TV and there he was: Otis Robbins. The reporter who was also on our TV, lamenting the sad state of affairs when an American was allowed to marry into the British royal family.

"He's the one who gave the kidnap order?" I asked.

"Yes, yes, yes!" cried Sweetie. "How many times do I have to repeat myself?"

"I would recognize that guy everywhere," said Molly.

"But you said he was blond," I said.

"Well, he is," said Sweetie. "Sort of."

"He's dark-haired," said Fräulein decidedly. "With gray streaks. Just as I said."

"Oh, why do you always have to be right?" Molly grumbled.

"Because I am?"

"Gran, he's the one," I said. "He's the one who had us kidnapped. And I'll bet he's also the one who's been trying to kill Tessa."

"But he wasn't anywhere near the house when that poisoned tea was served," said Gran.

"So he must be working with someone on the inside," I said. "That's why he was hanging around the cottage. He was meeting his associate."

"Suzy," said Gran.

And that's when we heard a noise.

"What was that?" asked the Queen, visibly perturbed.

"I don't know," said Gran. "It came from your grandson's room."

"Can you please check? I've been worried sick about those two. I know they haven't told me everything, and I can't help feeling something is going on."

"You're right," said Gran. "Someone's been trying to kill Tessa."

"I knew it!" said the Queen. "Vesta, you have to stop them!"

"Oh, don't worry, Lizzie, I will," said Gran as she rushed to the door of Dante and Tessa's room.

She burst inside, followed by Dooley and me. The sight that met our eyes was shocking to say the least: Tessa's cousin Nesbit was aiming a gun at Tessa, while Dante stood in a corner of the room, his hands behind his head.

CHAPTER 34

"Come on in," said Nesbit, turning the gun to cover Gran now.

"Oh, dear," I could hear the Queen say. Nesbit hadn't heard, though.

Gran held up her hands, aiming the phone at Nesbit, so the Queen had a first-row seat to the proceedings. Dooley and I were on the floor, and I don't think the security man even noticed us. Isn't that often the case, though?

"Close the door behind you, that's a nice old lady," said the guy.

Gran kicked the door closed with such force the guy winced.

"If you don't want the kid to get it, you'll do exactly as I say," he said, aiming the gun at Silvy now. Tessa protectively cradled the child in her arms, eliciting a grimace from her cousin.

"How could you?" she asked. "You're family!"

"I could ask you the same thing. Ever since you married this ginger bozo you haven't exactly shared the wealth, have you? You're living in luxury, enjoying carrot top's fortune while the rest of your family has to struggle to make ends meet."

"I gave you a job."

"Yeah, working as your messenger boy," he scoffed. "You're a big disappointment to all of us, Tessa. But then I should have known. You always were as tightfisted and self-centered as your mother."

If looks could kill, the guy would have been dead.

"You're making a big mistake," said Dante.

"No, I'm finally making my connection to Tessa pay off."

"How is my death going to pay off for you?" she asked.

"I thought you'd never ask."

"He's working with Otis Robbins," said Gran. "The two of them are in this together."

"Aren't you the smartest one in the room!" said the guy. "Yeah, Otis and I met in the pub late one night and got to talking. We soon discovered we shared a mutual hobby: hating on Tessa. He'd been snubbed by her, when he asked for an exclusive interview, and so had I. So after a couple of pints of lager he came up with a brilliant idea: he was going to write a book revealing all of Tess's deepest, darkest secrets and he wanted me to provide the material.

"You know, the kind of stuff only a loving cousin who's known Tessa all her life would know about. And then I did him one better: I said the best way to guarantee the book's success was for its subject to die. He thought I was joking but I wasn't. It's the only way for her to pay for the neglect and the hardship she's caused us all. So we made a pact, only half in jest: I would kill Tessa and he would write his tell-all book and we'd split the proceeds fifty-fifty."

"That's horrible, Nesbit," said Tessa, shaking her head.

"I think it's pretty clever. And I'm sure the rest of the family will agree."

"Are they in on this, too?"

"Nope. Just me. I guess that makes me the smart one, huh?"

"I think it makes you an asshat," said Gran.

Nesbit grinned. "You got a potty mouth, granny."

"You ain't heard nothing yet, sonny boy. Now put down that gun."

"Not a chance." He switched the gun to cover Dante. "So who wants to go first? Prince Charming over there? Or the People's Princess?"

"You're going to make it look like a murder-suicide, aren't you?" said Gran.

"Boom! The lady is on fire!"

"So how are you going to explain about me?"

"Collateral damage. When Dante went nuts and decided to kill his wife, his baby and turn the gun on himself, you were in the wrong place at the wrong time."

"Noooo!" Tessa cried, aghast when the depravity of her cousin came home to her.

"Don't do this," Dante growled, and took a step towards Nesbit.

"Not so fast, Prince. Back off!"

I had a feeling that the scenario didn't just look bleak for the humans in the room, but for Dooley and me, too. If this man didn't blink at taking four human lives, he would mind even less about two cats who just happened to be on the scene. If he noticed us, of course, which until then he still hadn't.

The thing is, cats aren't dogs. We don't have the superlative biting power in our maws the way some dogs do. One thing we do have are very sharp claws and some very sharp teeth. And hey, we don't mind using them. We stem from the jungle cat, you see, and I wasn't going to let this loser murder my precious human just because he wanted to make a quick buck.

So while the guy was gabbing away as if there was no tomorrow, Dooley and I locked eyes. We were going to teach this little piggy a lesson he wouldn't forget. Only one thing gave me pause: he was holding that gun. And if we launched ourselves at him he would probably fire off a shot. Chances were he was going to hit someone in that room. And we couldn't very well have that.

And then, as if she'd read my mind, suddenly the voice of the Queen boomed through the room, imperious and decisive.

"Nesbit Seller, put down that gun at once!"

"What the hell?!" said the guy, looking as if he'd just heard a ghost.

"This is your Queen speaking," said the Queen, and when Gran turned the phone so the guy could see the Queen's face, his jaw dropped a few inches.

And so did the gun…

"Now, Dooley!" I cried, and we both launched ourselves at the man. I went for the face while Dooley went for the man's gun hand. We landed simultaneously and while I clung to the man's visage, digging my claws in while I hissed up a storm, Dooley sank his teeth into the man's hand.

I can assure you—it was not pretty. The man shrieked like a piglet.

The gun must have dropped from his hand, for he tried to wrench us off with both hands. But cats are like the Canadian Mounties. We always get our man! And we don't let go, no matter what.

"Max, Dooley," suddenly a soft voice spoke.

It was the most wondrous sound in the world. The sound of my human.

"You can let go now," said Odelia.

And so we did.

EPILOGUE

a week after the harrowing time we'd lived through at Newtmore Cottage, we were in Scotland, enjoying a leisurely time at Balmoral Castle, the Queen's favorite getaway.

The royal Numero Uno had invited us all up there to recover from the shock of the recent events. Tessa and Dante were there, along with Angela. Jeremy and Jennie had also arrived, with the kids, and the Queen had organized an actual feast in her backyard, complete with a grill for one of the guests of honor: none other than Tex, who'd been flown in on the Queen's private jet with Marge and Alec. In other words: the gang was together again.

Tex, aided and abetted by one of the Queen's very own chefs, was flipping burgers on the grill, while the rest of the family had put its feet under the table. The Queen—or Lizzie to us—was enjoying some leisurely time with her kids, grandkids and great-grandkids, while the rest enjoyed the great food.

Meanwhile, a separate table had been set up for the pets, which comprised Dooley and me, Harriet and Brutus, Fluffy, of course, and the Queen's corgis, who had since become a little less frosty about the prospect of breathing the same air as cats. Though they still didn't seem entirely happy about sitting at the same table with us.

"So is it true you guys attacked the bad man?" asked Sweetie.

"That's right," I said. "I went for the face and Dooley went for his gun."

"That's the way to do it," growled Fräulein, punching the air with her paw.

On the table in front of us the most delicious food had been set out. Liver pâté, peanut butter and bacon treats, organic chicken strips, cat donuts with bacon sprinkles and lots and lots more. A regular royal feast!

"We couldn't have done it without you, though," I said.

"The moment I saw that guy, I said, that's the kidnapper!" Molly cried.

"But why did the Queen suddenly decide to get on the phone with Tessa?" asked Harriet. "That's what I don't understand."

"She must have realized that what we were yapping about was significant," said Sweetie. "And she wanted to talk to a fellow dog person."

"The Queen understands us," said Fräulein. "I don't know how she does it, but it's true."

"You mean the Queen can talk to her pets, like our humans can?" asked Dooley.

"I'm not absolutely certain, but she is very intuitive. Like when I fell through that hole in the ice last winter. She knew something was wrong, and she'd fished me out of that pond before I was going down for the third time."

"The Queen is amazing," Sweetie confirmed. "She is. She loves all her animals, from her Shetland ponies to her horses to her corgis to the bagpipes that wake her up every morning."

"Bagpipes are an instrument, not an animal," Fräulein pointed out.

"But she loves her subjects more, right?" said Harriet.

"The three corgis laughed. "I wouldn't be too sure!" said Fräulein.

"Well, I'm glad it's all over," said Fluffy. "The tension was killing me. It's no fun knowing that there's someone out there trying to kill your mistress."

"I can only imagine," said Fräulein, shaking her head. "That must have been terrible for you."

"It was," confirmed Fluffy. "And if it hadn't been for these hero cats, the bad guys would have succeeded, and I'd be an orphan now."

The dogs all stared at us, then Sweetie said, holding up a piece of chicken, "I think it's high time we salute these brave cats."

All paws went up, and then Fräulein said, "From now on we declare you honorary dogs."

I grimaced. It's not a big honor to be an honorary dog, I meant to say. But I'm sure they meant well, so we all smiled and thanked them profusely.

Tessa's cousin had been arrested, though later we were told he needed stitches, which actually gave me a twinge of pride. His associate Otis Robbins had also been arrested, and both men were going away for a long time, to a place called Belmarsh, which didn't have the same ring to it as the Tower.

The Queen had come down in person that night, without her corgis, and made Tessa and Dante promise that next time something like this happened, they had to tell her immediately, and not keep anything from her ever again.

She'd also invited us up to Balmoral, and told Gran she might not be able to become Queen of America, but she was always welcome to visit so they could chat over tea. I'd never seen Gran so over the moon as in that moment.

We spent a couple of days in London, seeing the sights, or at least the humans did, and then we all traveled down to Scotland on the Queen's personal train—yes, the Queen has her own private train!—so here we were.

Gran wandered over to our table. "Now isn't this the life?" she said with a wistful sigh. We were leaving for Hampton Cove next week, and I could tell she would have preferred to stick around for a couple of weeks more.

"It's pretty sweet," I agreed.

"Lizzie is going to make me a dame," said Gran. "Can you believe it? Dame Vesta Muffin. Wait till I tell my friends back home. Wait till I tell Scarlett!"

Scarlett Canyon is Gran's nemesis. And the fact that she could upstage her probably meant more to Gran than all possible royal honors combined.

Odelia and Chase also wandered over, accompanied by Marge, Tex and Uncle Alec.

"You guys did great," said Odelia, not for the first time. "And so did you," she said as she held up her glass in a salute to the corgis.

"Aw," said Sweetie, in an uncharacteristic display of modesty.

"See?" said Gran. "The Queen of England has her corgis, the Queen of America has her cats, and together they make history."

A voice startled Gran. "Did I hear my name?" the Queen asked.

"I was just saying how one can tell a real queen from a fake one by the way she communicates with her pets," said Gran.

The Queen smiled. "It's true! Like the night we caught that nasty Otis Robbins. The moment that horrid man filled the screen with his horrible visage, Sweetie, Fräulein and Molly told me immediately. 'That's the one!' they said. 'That's the man who kidnapped us!' So naturally the first thought that popped into my head was that I had to warn dear Tessa. Luckily you were there to pick up the phone and the rest, as they say, is history!"

"Is this going to be in the history books?" asked Tex, curious.

"I doubt it," said the Queen. "No one would believe it. And the ones that do would think their precious monarch had gone a little soft in the head."

"But... you can actually talk to your dogs?" asked Chase.

The Queen smiled enigmatically. "Is that so hard to believe?" she said, and walked off.

Stunned, the others all stared after her.

"I knew it," said Gran. "I just knew it! And that's why I need to be crowned Queen of America!"

"Yeah, that'll happen," said Uncle Alec.

"Now don't be a Negative Ned, Alec," said Gran. "It will happen because I want it to happen."

"It would definitely be an improvement," said Marge.

Tex raised both eyebrows. He clearly wasn't in agreement.

"Would that mean you have to move to Washington?" asked Dooley.

"Of course. I'd have to move into the White House. You'll all be invited to stay, of course. I'll make sure there's plenty of space for the whole family."

Tex was smiling now, the prospect of his mother-in-law finally moving out of the house doing much to warm him to the prospect of calling her Queen.

"I would like to live in the White House," said Harriet. "And be First Cat."

"I think I'd be First Cat, though," said Brutus. "I am the most handsome."

"Obviously the First Cat would be the prettiest cat," said Harriet with a laugh. "In other words: me."

"I think the First Cat should be a hero," said Brutus. "Someone like me."

"And I think the First Cat should look good on Instagram."

"The First Cat should be butch. An inspiration to all the cats in America."

"Oh, give me a break," said Harriet. "You? An inspiration? As if."

"Oh, dear," said Marge. "Here we go again."

"What are they talking about?" asked Chase.

"They're arguing about who gets to be First Cat once Gran becomes America's queen," said Odelia.

They all laughed, even though for Brutus and Harriet it was clearly no laughing matter.

"You both get to be First Cats," said Gran. "We'll do it in rotation."

Tessa and Dante now joined us, Tessa carrying the baby. "Having a good time?" said Tessa with a smile.

"A great time, thanks," said Odelia gratefully.

"I can't thank you guys enough. I'll never forget this."

"The queen is giving us all honorary KBEs," said Odelia. "Which is so great."

"Yeah, I asked her," said Dante. "No one deserves it more than you."

'Wait, you're *all* going to be dames and knights?" asked Gran, appalled.

Odelia and Chase nodded. "Yup," said Angela. "I'm going to be a dame, too. Can you imagine? When I tell my friends they won't believe me."

"Oh, for crying out loud!" Gran said, shaking her fist.

And as the humans drifted off to scoop some more food

onto their plates, Dooley said, "Do you think they'll make us dames and knights too, Max?"

"I doubt it," I said. "That seems to be a thing for humans only."

"She'll do you one better," said Fräulein.

"Yeah, she told us she'll give you all PBEs," said Sweetie.

"What's a PBE?" I asked.

"Pet of the Order of the British Empire," Fräulein explained. "It's a secret society the Queen launched shortly after her coronation. Only the bravest pets are members. And all of her corgis, of course. Now you'll be inducted, too."

Sweetie gave us a warm smile. "You know what? You've earned it—all of you."

"Did you hear that, Max?" said Dooley. "We're going to be knighted!"

"Well, congratulations, Sir Dooley," I said.

"Why, thank you, Sir Max," he said.

It certainly took the sting out of being kicked out of cat choir. Shanille might even take me back now. She was a sucker for all things royal.

"First Cat *and* a knight," Brutus grunted. "Sweet."

Harriet produced a feeble whimper. We all looked at her. She was biting her lip, clearly worried about something.

"Aren't you happy, Harriet?" I asked. "This is a huge honor."

She gave me an apologetic smile. "I just wonder where they'll pin the badge and ribbon."

Ouch!

EXCERPT FROM PURRFECT CUT
(THE MYSTERIES OF MAX 14)

Chapter One

A bashful sun was playing peekaboo over the horizon and distributing its first timid rays upon a restful world when I woke up. As usual I'd been dozing at the foot of my human's bed after having spent the first part of the night exploring the ultimate range of my singing voice. As you may or may not know, I've long been a member of Hampton Cove's cat choir, pride of our small town, where cats can still be cats and sing their little hearts out. Only Shanille, our stalwart and earnest conductor, had recently kicked me out of the choir, on account of the fact that several of the members had complained about my abject failure to carry a tune. The incident had greatly saddened me, as you can well imagine, since I've always been a staunch proponent of cats' rights to express themselves in song. So when my membership card was withdrawn I must confess it shook me to the very core of my being.

Fortunately I'm not the kind of cat who takes life's vicissitudes lying down, so to speak, even though ironically enough

I do spend a great portion of my life lying down, and soon I was practicing hard to make a triumphant return.

Last night offered me the first opportunity since returning from England, where my human's adventures had taken us, to showcase my progress. And to my elation Shanille and the other members—even those whose complaints had terminated my contract in the first place—deemed me fit for duty once more.

So it was with renewed fervor that I rejoined the choir's rank and file, and I won't conceal the fact that the whole thing gave me a distinct sense that all was well in my world, and upon ending last night's rehearsal, I practically skipped along the road, extremely pleased with myself and my progress.

It isn't too much to say that the mood was festive, so my friends and I decided to paint this small town of ours red, and Brutus led us along all of his favorite haunts, like a nice little rooftop restaurant that keeps the bins out where we can reach them, and our gang of four—myself, Dooley, Harriet and of course Brutus—experienced an enjoyable night on the town. It was only understandable, then, that I felt the need to sleep in. It was with a slight sense of annoyance, therefore, that I greeted the rising sun, which had decided to cut my extended slumber short by spreading its light across a peaceful world.

I stretched and yawned cavernously, as is my habit, and glanced around in search of Dooley, who usually likes to fall asleep next to me. Once upon a time we used to have a big chunk of the bed all to ourselves, but that was before Odelia decided to hook up with a burly policeman who answers to the name Chase Kingsley, and asked him to move in with her. Nowadays the bed is a little cramped for two humans and two cats, which tends to create a touch of awkwardness. The issue isn't Odelia, who's a fairly shortish human being, so her feet don't invade the stretch of bed I like to call my own. What's more, she tends to curl up into a ball when she sleeps—the fetus position I think experts like to call it—which adds to my acreage. No, the problem is Chase, who's one of those long and stretchy humans, and likes to stick his feet where they don't belong: in our territory. I've mentioned this to Odelia, and she's promised to have a talk with the invasive cop, but until then it's tough for a cat to find the space to sleep in peace. Especially since Chase is not one of your more peaceful sleepers. The man tends to toss and turn, and even lash out when the mood strikes, giving poor Dooley the occasional kick in the tail end.

I guess scientists who claim that people sleeping in separate beds enjoy a deeper, better sleep are on to something. All I know is that if only Chase would sleep in a separate bed, we'd all be better off—or at least I would.

Yes, I know I can always sleep on the couch, and I also know there are several other spots at my disposal. Like Marge and Tex's bed. But Odelia's parents' bed is already spoken for, by Brutus and Harriet, and even they have confided in me they suffer the same fate Dooley and I do, with Tex being one of those stringbeany types, whose highly-strung feet seem to have a mind of their own. Dooley, of course, is in the best position of all: he can choose to sleep at Odelia's, or Grandma's. Why he chooses Odelia's is beyond me. She's not technically his human, and still he spends all of his nights here. Then again, it's comforting to have my best friend and wingman nearby, and perhaps he feels the same way, which is why he endures Chase's nervous footwork, and so do I.

I opened one eye, then the other, and saw that Odelia was awake already. Oddly enough she was staring at Chase, who was still fast asleep. So I elbowed Dooley in the tummy and he muttered something that didn't sound entirely friendly.

"Check this out," I whispered. "Odelia is making a study of Chase."

Dooley reluctantly dragged his heavy eyelids open and stared in the direction indicated.

"Huh," he said finally. "Weird."

"Right?"

We both watched on as Odelia watched, with a strange look on her face, the sleeping cop.

"I don't get it," said Dooley. "What's the big attraction?"

"I have no idea," I confessed.

"It's just a sleeping human."

"It is, and he's not even looking his best."

Chase, who some people claim is a handsome fellow, with one of those chiseled faces, strong jaws and long, brown hair, doesn't look his best in the morning. His trademark mane is usually tousled, and more often than not there's a tiny thread of drool visibly at the corner of his mouth. Not exactly the kind of face that would successfully grace the cover of a romance novel. Then again, Odelia's features aren't much to write home about either. Her fair hair is usually a mess, and she develops weird sleep marks on her fine-boned face.

"I mean, if you've seen one sleeping human, you've seen them all," I said.

"It's love," suddenly a third party entered the discussion.

Dooley and I looked up in surprise, to discover that Harriet had joined us. She must have jumped up onto the bed while we were chatting, and was now gazing upon the peaceful scene with a strange little smile on her furry face.

"Love?" I said. "Um, I don't think so. I think she's counting the pores on his nose. And judging from the time it's taking her there are a lot of them."

"Or the stubble on his cheeks," said Dooley. "The man has a lot of stubble."

"Exactly," I said. "Lots of stubble and lots of pores so plenty to look at."

"Oh, you silly, silly boys," said Harriet good-naturedly. "Can't you see Odelia is in love and is simply drinking in the sheer beauty of her beloved?"

I studied the scene with this new information in mind. "Nope," I said finally. "I don't see it."

"That's because you've never been in love," said Harriet curtly.

"Oh, I've been in love," I said. "I've been in love plenty of times. But even then I didn't stare at the face of my beloved like some doofus."

"Odelia is not a doofus," said Harriet. "She's a woman in love, and that's what a woman in love looks like when faced with the object of her affection."

I studied Odelia more closely. Her lips were curved in a tiny smile, her half-lidded eyes sparkled, and a blush mantled her cheeks. All in all she looked a little dopey. As if she needed to go poo-poo and didn't want to wake up Chase.

"I think she needs to go wee-wee and she's afraid to wake him," said Dooley, proving that we were kindred spirits.

Harriet rolled her eyes in that expressive way only she can pull off.

"Ugh. You guys are so dumb," she said.

"It's obvious," said Dooley. "And I can't believe you can't see it."

"Apart from the fact that I think she needs to go poo-poo and not wee-wee, Dooley is right," I said. "This is obviously a woman who is silently praying for her boyfriend to finally wake up so she can make a run for the bathroom."

"I'm telling you it's love! How can you confuse love with having to go wee-wee or poo-poo!" Odelia uttered a little sigh, and the three of us looked up. "See?" said Harriet triumphantly. "Only a person in love can produce such a delightful little sigh."

"It's the sigh of a woman who needs to go pee-pee and knows she can't go," said Dooley, sticking to his guns.

Suddenly a deep, rumbling voice echoed through the room. "When are those darned cats going to shut up?" The voice was Chase's and obviously, in spite of our best efforts, we hadn't been as quiet and respectful as we'd hoped.

"Finally," I said. "He's awake. Now Odelia can stop counting his pores and his stubble and go to the bathroom."

"A bowl of kibble says they're going to snuggle," said Harriet. "Because snuggling is what humans in love always do."

"You're on," I said. "A bowl of kibble says she's going to take this opportunity to make a run for the bathroom."

But we were both disappointed, and the bet would have to remain a toss-up. For at that exact moment the front doorbell jangled, and both Odelia and Chase uttered a groan of annoyance and made to get up and start their day.

Unfortunately Chase did this with a little less tact and care than Odelia, and the upshot was that his sudden movements bumped Harriet from the bed and onto the carpeted floor, then also sent Dooley flying. The only one still in position was me, and I carefully watched Odelia as she swung her feet to the floor. "A bowl of kibble says Chase will go downstairs to open the door and Odelia is going to race to the bathroom," I said, still wanting to win my bet.

Three pairs of cat's eyes watched carefully as two humans stuck their feet into their respective slippers—a pair of Hello Kitty slippers for Odelia and boring old brown ones for Chase—and got up. They both moved out of the room, but before reaching the door Chase took a sharp left turn and muttered, "Can you get that, babe? I need to take a wee." And before she had the chance to respond, he'd closed the bathroom door behind him and that was that.

Talk about a shock twist! Which just goes to show that human behavior is very hard to predict indeed.

"All bets are off," said Dooley, sounding disappointed.

"And we still don't know why Odelia was staring at Chase's face for the best part of an hour," I added, equally disappointed.

"Love!" Harriet cried as she padded to the door. "I keep telling you. Love!"

"Yeah, right," I said. Only a female feline could come up with a dumb theory like that. Dooley and I exchanged a knowing glance. We were in agreement: Harriet was crazy. And we didn't even need to bet kibble over that. It was a fact, borne out by long association with the white-haired Persian.

And since we were all up now we decided to follow in Odelia's footsteps and see who this early morning visitor could be. Even before we'd set paw on the first step of the stairs, I recognized the voice of Odelia's uncle Alec, Hampton Cove's police chief and generally a harbinger of bad news.

"Uh-oh," I said. "This can't be good."

We hurried down the stairs, all questions regarding human behavior wiped from our minds. And as we arrived in the living room, the first words I heard were, "He was dead when we got there. Dead as a dodo."

I heaved a deep sigh. I may not know why humans like to stare at one another in the early morning, but here's one thing I do know: humans simply can't seem to stop murdering each other. The good thing, of course, is that this unseemly habit provides a steady flow of income for the fine upstanding men and women employed by the Hampton Cove Police Department. And Odelia.

I probably should have mentioned this before, but Odelia

is by way of being a local sleuthhound. Officially she's a reporter for the *Hampton Cove Gazette*, but her natural curiosity and keen intelligence have turned her into something of a local amateur detective. And that's where the four of us come in. As cats we have access to all those places that are usually off-limits even to your intrepid reporter-slash-sleuth. Places only cats can sneak into unseen and unheard, and pick up those precious tidbits of information that are not designed for snooping eyes and ears. Plus, we get to talk to all the other cats that freely roam our town, along with its resident animal population, wild or domesticated, large or small. And it provides us what a pretty accurate picture of what goes on in our town at all times, which we then dutifully convey to Odelia, and which has helped her solve numerous crimes so far.

I know they say cats are selfish and solitary creatures, and if a human wants to choose a partner from the animal kingdom they should pick a dog. Well, that's where they would be wrong. Dogs, because of their natural tendency to shoot their mouths off and trip over their own clumsy feet, are the worst sidekick imaginable. If you really want to get the job done, you should pick a cat. Discreet, silent as the night, and naturally nosy, we are the perfect amateur sleuth's assistant, and that isn't merely my humble opinion. It's a fact.

"So who's dead?" asked Odelia, stifling a yawn.

Uncle Alec, a ruddy-faced man with russet sideburns and only a few token hairs left on top of his head, cocked an eyebrow. "Have you ever heard of Leonidas Flake?"

Odelia frowned. "The fashion designer?"

Uncle Alec nodded. "That's the one."

"He died?"

"He died," the portly police chief confirmed. "And what's more, we know exactly who did it."

"Who?"

"Gabriel Crier. His partner of thirty years. We found him with the bloody knife in his hands, bent over the corpse of his dead lover."

"If you know who did it, then why are you here?" Odelia asked.

He shrugged. "I just figured you'd like to have the scoop."

Odelia's face twisted into a wide smile. "I love you, Uncle Alec."

"I know you do. Now where the hell is Chase? I've been trying to call him all morning."

Chapter Two

Chase joined his boss and Odelia in the kitchen. Odelia had made the three of them a pot of her trademark strong coffee and they were now sipping from the tasty black brew, accompanied by toasted waffles for Uncle Alec, yogurt for Odelia, and a bowl of cereal for Chase.

"You should watch that stuff," said Odelia, pointing to the warm waffle her uncle was devouring.

Alec blinked. "Watch the waffle?" he stared at the thing as if expecting some bug to come crawling out.

"It contains a lot of bad stuff. Palm oil, for one thing. And you know what palm oil does for your cholesterol, Uncle Alec."

He stared at her. "Um, no, I don't."

"It's bad for you, all right? Just... try not to eat too much of it."

He gave her a sheepish nod, then shoved the rest of his waffle home. He'd sprayed a liberal helping of whipped cream from the can on top of it, and now licked the remnants from his fingers. There were a lot of people in Alec's life who tried to make him eat the right thing, and who had taken it upon themselves to alter his diet for the better. Only problem was,

Uncle Alec was a bachelor, and what he did in the sanctity of his own home was nobody's business but his own, an opinion he stuck to diligently. Chase had lived with the big guy for a while, and seen firsthand the kind of diet the Chief kept. Many were the nights the two of them had sat on the big couch in Alec's living room, watching a game on the big TV and shoving down burgers, slices of pepperoni pizza and chips. Washed down with beer, it added to the impressive belly the police chief had managed to construct around his midsection.

Good thing, at least, that he usually ate his dinners at his sister Marge's place, who made sure her brother got some wholesome nourishment in him.

"So if this fashion designer was killed with a knife," said Odelia, "and his boyfriend was found standing over him with that same knife clutched in his hand, blood all over him, has he confessed to the crime already?"

"Funny you should ask that," said Uncle Alec. "No, he hasn't."

Odelia cut a glance to her boyfriend, who'd risen from the table and was now engaged in his favorite morning ritual of preparing a protein shake to take into the office. "So... he's claiming to be innocent or what?" asked Chase.

"Not exactly," said Alec, digging a knife into the pot of Nutella and applying an ample spread to his next waffle and ignoring Odelia's look of concern. "He has no recollection of the crime."

"What do you mean?" asked Odelia.

"He has no idea how he got there, how the knife got into his hand, and how his dead boyfriend got dead in the first place. Complete blackout."

"Who is this Gabriel Crier anyway?" asked Chase.

Alec took his little notebook from his front shirt pocket and flipped it open. He cleared his throat noisily. "Gabriel

Jake Crier. Fifty-four. Worked as a hairstylist to the stars for a while, before meeting Leonidas Flake at an art show in Paris and becoming his personal hairdresser and then something more."

"How old was Leonidas?" asked Odelia, gratefully accepting the protein shake Chase had just mixed up.

"Um, seventy-eight, and still going strong by all accounts," said Alec, kindly refusing a similar offer.

"It's good for you," Odelia pointed out. "Drink it. You'll like it. It's a vitamin bomb and you'll feel much better."

"It tastes like horse piss."

Instead of being insulted, Chase laughed loudly. "And how would you know what horse piss tastes like?"

"I don't have to taste it to know what it tastes like," said Alec, with the kind of strange logic the unhealthy use to remain unhealthy. He took a pack of cigarettes from his other front shirt pocket and shook one out.

Odelia watched on in horror. "Don't tell me you started smoking again!"

"No, I haven't," he said. "But I can't seem to shake the habit of taking one out of the pack from time to time." And as he said it, he put the cigarette to his lips. He smiled a beatific smile. "Feels so good," he muttered, then grudgingly put it away again and returned the pack to his shirt pocket. "Where were we?"

"So Gabriel Crier worked for Leonidas Flake as his personal hairstylist and something more?" Chase prompted as he licked the green sludge from his lips.

"Right. He was also rumored to be the designer's right-hand man."

"As a fashion designer?" asked Odelia.

"Was he any good?"

"Who knows," said the chief with a sigh. "I know about as

much about fashion as the next chief of police." He tucked away his little notebook.

"Maybe he felt things weren't moving along fast enough?" Odelia said. "And so he figured if he killed his boyfriend he'd become the new top guy?"

"Yeah, but that's just it. I talked to the guy's attorney early this morning. As far as he knows the most recent will and testament doesn't exactly hand the keys to the kingdom to the boyfriend. On the contrary. Everything goes to—"

"The kids?" Chase offered.

"Siblings?" Odelia guessed.

"—his cat," said Uncle Alec with a quick look towards the living room couch, where four cats sat listening to the kitchen counter conversation—Brutus had joined his friends, who had all made themselves comfortable.

"What?" asked Chase with a laugh. "A cat is inheriting the Leonidas Flake empire?"

"Looks like," said Alec. "Unless Mr. Flake made a last-minute change his attorney isn't aware of—and this seems very unlikely—the cat gets everything. The millions, the brand, the stores, the global fashion empire."

Odelia frowned. "I don't get it. How can a cat inherit a company?"

"Yeah, a cat can't run a business, can it?" said Chase, directing his question at Odelia, just to be on the safe side. She was, after all, the feline expert.

"I guess a cat could run a company," she said slowly, "if that cat knew a thing or two about business. But they would still have to relay all of the decisions through a human, who would then have to organize the actual day-to-day running of the business along those instructions. It would require a person who could intuit the cat's decision-making process, of course."

"A person like you, you mean," said Chase, who'd recently

been made aware of the fact that his fiancée was one of those rare people who could actually communicate with cats.

She nodded.

Chase turned to Alec. "And did Flake have such a person on the payroll?"

"That was Gabriel's task," he said. "He was in charge of Pussy's routine. Pussy being the name of Flake's cat. Mr. Crier took Pussy to her weekly visits to the pet salon, kept a close eye on her diet, organized her parties—"

"Sorry, her parties?" asked Chase.

"Yes, apparently this Pussy has a very busy social life, and as a rule Mr. Crier planned a lot of activities for her—she had a full schedule."

"Who told you all this stuff?" asked Odelia.

Alec dragged a meaty paw through the devastated area that was his scalp. "You'd be surprised how chatty staff members of the recently departed can be."

"You should have called," said Chase. "I would have helped set up the interviews."

"I did call you," said Uncle Alec. "And Odelia."

Both Odelia and Chase grabbed for their phones. "Shoot," Chase muttered. "Must have forgotten to plug the darn thing in last night."

"Same here," said Odelia, taking Chase's phone and proceeding to plug in both phones so they could recharge before they left the house.

"Anyway, it's a slam-dunk case," said Alec, eagerly checking out the uneaten waffle on his niece's plate and gratefully accepting it when she handed it to him. "Crier was caught red-handed, so I'm guessing we'll be done with this before lunch. Still, always good to cross our T's and dot our I's."

"Weird that the only person who stands to gain from the

designer's death is the man's cat," said Chase. "What do you make of that, Chief?"

He lowered his bristly brows into a frown. "Not sure, buddy. But you have to allow for the fact that these are celebrities, and as we all know celebrities are eccentric. Leonidas only changed his will last week. The one before that had the boyfriend as the main beneficiary, so there's always a chance he didn't know Flake cut him out of his will."

"I think the cat did it," Chase quipped.

"Funny guy," the Chief grumbled.

Odelia glanced over to her cats, who were listening attentively. "Did you hear that, you guys? Looks like we have a feline suspect for this one."

"Impossible," said Max. "A cat would never kill a human."

"I'm not so sure," said Brutus. "If that human treated him or her badly, anything is possible."

"But he was stabbed with a knife," Max pointed out. "Cats don't stab people with knives, Brutus."

"Cats don't need knives," said Harriet. "We use our inbuilt tools." And she unsheathed a razor-sharp claw to turn her words into a show-and-tell.

"Was he stabbed with the knife Crier was holding?" asked Odelia now.

"Um… not sure," said Alec. "Abe is delayed." He checked his watch. "He should be there shortly, though, so I better start heading back over there."

Odelia jumped down from the kitchen stool. "You mean to say the body is still there? The coroner hasn't even examined the victim?"

"Nope," said Alec with faux cheer. "Which is why I figured I might as well pick up you two, so you can give me a hand wrapping this thing up."

"We better get going," said Odelia. "I can't believe we've been sitting here chatting while that poor man is lying there."

"He's not going anywhere," said Alec, buttering a piece of toast.

"And I haven't taken a shower yet," said Odelia, patting her hair.

"You look fine," said Chase.

"Oh, God," she muttered. She hated leaving the house without taking a shower or putting on a fresh set of threads. "Give me five minutes."

"You can take ten," said Uncle Alec, unconcerned.

She hurried up the stairs, and took the quickest shower in the history of mankind, put on a pair of jeans, pulled a T-shirt and sweater over her head, and decided to forgo drying her hair for once, then hurried down again.

Alec and Chase were still chatting away, not a care in the world.

"Cats don't frame humans," Uncle Alec was saying. "That's a fact. I mean, no offense to you guys," he added, gesturing to Max and the others, "but I don't think you have it in you to try and frame someone for a crime you committed. Am I right or am I right?"

"Cats may be a lot of things but we're not that cunning," Brutus agreed.

"I wouldn't be too sure about that," said Harriet. "Cats can be very, very cunning."

"What is he saying, honey?" asked Alec.

"He's saying cats are not that cunning," said Odelia, shoving her notebook into her purse and checking the kitchen to see if all the appliances were turned off.

"And then there's the logistics of the thing," said Chase. "How would a cat kill a person, then plant the knife into the hand of another person, without that person's knowledge? It can't be done. No, I think you're right, Alec. The case is open-and-shut. All we need to do is get a confession and we're done."

201

"That's the plan," said Alec. He got down from the kitchen stool and hoisted up his pants. "Well, let's get going, kids. Chateau Leonidas awaits us."

"Chateau Leonidas?" asked Chase. "Why am I not surprised that the man lived in an actual castle?"

"Because if you're one of the most successful designers in the world, of course you live in a castle," said Alec. "Besides, he's French, so there's that."

"Do all French people live in castles?" asked Dooley.

"No, I don't think they do, Dooley," said Odelia with a smile. "Only the very wealthy."

"Oh," said Dooley, looking slightly disappointed.

"I, for one, can't wait to meet this Pussy," said Brutus with relish, then, when he caught Harriet's sideways glance, quickly added, "I mean, so we can talk to her, and find out what she knows."

Harriet, who'd narrowed her eyes, didn't seem all that excited at the prospect of meeting what could very well be the richest cat in the world. And as she extended and retracted her claws a few times, Odelia thought she could actually see Brutus's Adam's apple nervously shift up and down.

She hadn't even known cats actually had an Adam's apple.

Chapter Three

I glanced over to my feline comrades. It's one thing to act as a sleuthcat, but another to have to investigate a fellow cat for a crime they may or may not have committed. At least for me this marked the first occasion that a cat had been singled out as a possible suspect in a heinous crime like murder. Usually cats, when accused of a crime, are only guilty of misdemeanors like destroying a beloved set of curtains, a nice carpet here or there or stealing a fish from the fishmonger's slab. I've even known a cat who chased little chicks around the backyard of some minor amateur chicken farmer. When interviewed after the fact, he claimed to have been looking for a feathered little friend to play with.

"Cats can be killers, though," said Harriet seriously. "Cats have been known to kill birds and mice and on occasion even a rat or two."

"Cats kill fish," said Dooley, adding his two cents to the discussion.

"Don't talk nonsense," said Brutus brusquely. "Cats don't kill fish."

"They do!" said Dooley. "I once saw Shadow racing down Main Street with a complete fish between his teeth."

"I'm sure Shadow didn't catch that fish," said Harriet.

"No, he did," Dooley insisted. "He got it from Wilbur Vickery's store."

We all laughed, except for Dooley, who didn't seem to get the joke.

"That fish was already dead, Dooley," I said finally, when he merely stared at me, clearly expecting me to provide him with an explanation for the sudden chucklefest.

"Dead? I don't think so."

"Fish live in the sea," I said, "or in rivers or lakes or even the occasional pond. They don't hang around Wilbur Vickery's General Store."

"The fish Vickery sells is caught by fishermen," Harriet said. "Men who fish. In the sea," she added, as if addressing a not-so-clever kitten.

"Oh," said Dooley, clearly disappointed that his war story turned out to be a benign little tale instead. "Well, he did catch it, even if it was dead already."

"Just like I catch my kibble every day," Brutus said with a grin.

Harriet clapped her paws. "Order, people. Let's come to

order," she said. "Let's focus on the task at hand. We won't be able to help Odelia by telling tall tales of Shadow stealing fish from the General Store. We need to decide once and for all if cats are capable of homicide—in other words, the killing of a hominid."

"A what?" asked Brutus.

"A hominid. A member of the family of the Hominidae or great apes."

"A human," I explained.

"Oh, right," said Brutus.

"I once saw a story about a cat that likes to lie on top of its human's face," said Dooley. When we all stared at him, he added, "It was on the Discovery Channel so it must be true!"

"So did the human die?" asked Harriet.

"Yeah, that's the real issue here," Brutus added. "Did that human die?"

"I don't think so," said Dooley, frowning as he searched his memory. "No, I think he survived. At least he was alive when they interviewed him."

More eye rolls greeted Dooley's second contribution to our discussion, with some exasperated groans coming from Harriet, but once again it was up to me to explain to my dear friend what the problem was with his story.

"Dooley, if they interviewed the man after the fact, and he was able to recount the experience, he didn't die, see?"

He thought about this for a moment, then conceded, "No, I guess he didn't."

"Why did he lie on top of his human's face?" I asked, for the story did possess an element of intrigue.

"Yeah, did he try to kill him?" asked Brutus, who has a penchant for all things violent.

"No, I think he just wanted to show his affection," said Dooley. "Or maybe he was afraid his human's face would get cold during the night."

"Well, he shouldn't have," Harriet snapped. "Lying on top of a hominid's face might block certain aspects of the breathing apparatus and kill it dead."

"What's all this talk about hominids?" I asked.

"Marge loaned me an eBook she got from the library the other day," said Harriet. "Very interesting stuff. About the different species that make up this great big beautiful planet of ours. She felt I'd been spending too much time watching the Kardashians with Gran, and I should read something that would feed my mind instead. I like it. I might read a few more of them."

I was greatly surprised, but also greatly impressed. Harriet is not exactly known as the intellectual of our gang of four, and this was all to the good.

"Look, all this talk about killer cats is all well and good," said Brutus, "but frankly I don't buy it. Not for one second."

"What don't you buy?" asked Dooley, interested.

"That cats are capable of killing humans! It's simply not possible. I mean, they can claw their humans, when provoked, or even bite them, but kill them? I don't think any member of the feline species, in the long history we share with the human race, has ever been responsible for the death of a human."

"A cat could kill if it accidentally kicked over a candle and set the house on fire," Harriet pointed out.

"Yeah, but that's not exactly murder, is it? That's more like an accident."

"Brutus is right," I said. "What we need to ask ourselves is this: are cats capable of possessing the intent to kill? Willfully murder a human being?"

We all chewed on that one for a moment, then Dooley finally said, "Do you think Pussy is one of those cats that likes to wear booties?"

"Dooley, let's try to focus on the issue at hand for a

moment, shall we?" I said. "In a show of paws, who thinks cats are capable of manslaughter?"

No paws were raised. "Well, that settles it," said Harriet. "Pussy is innocent, and whoever claims she did what they say she did is lying through their teeth."

"We'll know more after we've talked to her," I said.

Odelia, who'd been surfing the internet, preparatory to launching her investigation, now called out, "Did you know that Leonidas was couturier to kings and queens and presidents?"

"No, I did not know that," I said, but when Chase joined her at the computer it dawned on me that her question hadn't actually been directed at me.

Instead, Chase said, "Well what do you know?"

I stared at my human for a moment, then back at my posse. They quickly looked away. It had been an embarrassing moment for me, and none of them wanted to rub my face in it. Which was nice of them, I guess. Then again, it highlighted a growing concern we all shared: ever since Chase had moved in, our face time with Odelia had gradually diminished to the point it had almost been reduced to zero. Used to be she spent all of her free time with us, or her family, who live right next door. These days she spends most of her time with Chase, and what little time is left, she devotes to taking care of our basic needs. It's been an adjustment, let me tell you, and one we're struggling with.

"It's all right, Maxie, baby," said Brutus finally. "It's happened to us all."

And it had, which meant it was turning into a serious problem. I mean, what good is it to be able to talk to your human, if that human is always busy talking to her significant other human? None whatsoever, right?

Anyway, I know I'm nagging and whining, which is so not me. Cats rarely nag and whine. At least not this cat. Still, being ignored by your favorite human in all the world is a tough one, and if I hadn't known better I'd have thought Odelia sometimes did it on purpose, to show us that things had changed around here. That we were no longer her top priority.

Just then Odelia and Chase moved to the door, then passed out into the street and we could hear the key being turned in the lock. Silence reigned for a moment, as we all stared at the closed door. Finally, Harriet spoke. "Correct me if I'm wrong, you guys. But did Odelia just forget to take us along?"

ABOUT NIC

Nic Saint is the pen name for writing couple Nick and Nicole Saint. They've penned novels in the romance, cat sleuth, middle grade, suspense, comedy and cozy mystery genres. Nicole has a background in accounting and Nick in political science and before being struck by the writing bug the Saints worked odd jobs around the world (including massage therapist in Mexico, gardener in Italy, restaurant manager in India, and Berlitz teacher in Belgium).

When they're not writing they enjoy Christmas-themed Hallmark movies (whether it's Christmas or not), all manner of pastry, comic books, a daily dose of yoga (to limber up those limbs), and spoiling their big red tomcat Tommy.

www.nicsaint.com

ALSO BY NIC SAINT

The Mysteries of Max
Purrfect Murder
Purrfectly Deadly
Purrfect Revenge
Box Set 1 (Books 1-3)
Purrfect Heat
Purrfect Crime
Purrfect Rivalry
Box Set 2 (Books 4-6)
Purrfect Peril
Purrfect Secret
Purrfect Alibi
Box Set 3 (Books 7-9)
Purrfect Obsession
Purrfect Betrayal
Purrfectly Clueless
Box Set 4 (Books 10-12)
Purrfectly Royal
Purrfect Cut
Purrfect Trap
Purrfectly Hidden
Purrfect Kill

Purrfect Santa
Purrfectly Flealess

Nora Steel

Murder Retreat

The Kellys

Murder Motel

Death in Suburbia

Emily Stone

Murder at the Art Class

Washington & Jefferson

First Shot

Alice Whitehouse

Spooky Times

Spooky Trills

Spooky End

Spooky Spells

Ghosts of London

Between a Ghost and a Spooky Place

Public Ghost Number One

Ghost Save the Queen

Box Set 1 (Books 1-3)

A Tale of Two Harrys

Ghost of Girlband Past

Ghostlier Things

Charleneland

Deadly Ride

Final Ride

Neighborhood Witch Committee

Witchy Start

Witchy Worries

Witchy Wishes

Saffron Diffley

Crime and Retribution

Vice and Verdict

Felonies and Penalties (Saffron Diffley Short 1)

The B-Team

Once Upon a Spy

Tate-à-Tate

Enemy of the Tates

Ghosts vs. Spies

The Ghost Who Came in from the Cold

Witchy Fingers

Witchy Trouble

Witchy Hexations

Witchy Possessions

Witchy Riches

Box Set 1 (Books 1-4)

The Mysteries of Bell & Whitehouse

One Spoonful of Trouble

Two Scoops of Murder

Three Shots of Disaster

Box Set 1 (Books 1-3)

A Twist of Wraith

A Touch of Ghost

A Clash of Spooks

Box Set 2 (Books 4-6)

The Stuffing of Nightmares

A Breath of Dead Air

An Act of Hodd

Box Set 3 (Books 7-9)

A Game of Dons

Standalone Novels

When in Bruges

The Whiskered Spy

ThrillFix

Homejacking

The Eighth Billionaire

The Wrong Woman

Made in the USA
Coppell, TX
23 December 2020

46972551R00132